THE Uncle Wiggily BOOK

By HOWARD R. GARIS

Illustrated by CARL and MARY HAUGE

GROSSET & DUNLAP · Publishers · NEW YORK

Uncle Wiggily and His Neighbors

Uncle Wiggily Longears, the rabbit gentleman, lives in Wood Land. He is always very kind and polite.

Nurse Jane Fuzzy Wuzzy is a muskrat lady. She keeps house for Uncle Wiggily.

Baby Bunty, a little rabbit girl, often plays tricks on Uncle Wiggily.

The sly Weasel lives in Wood Land, too. He tries to catch rabbits.

The Hawk is always hungry. He would catch Uncle Wiggily if he could.

Nannie Wagtail is a little goat girl. She helps her mother keep house. She has a brother named Billie.

Uncle Butter, the goat gentleman, is Uncle Wiggily's friend. He lives in Wood Land near the rabbit gentleman's home.

Jillie and Jolly Longtail are the mouse children. They have a little cousin named Squeakie Eekie.

The Bear is the biggest animal in Wood Land. Sometimes he gets into trouble when he tries to catch Uncle Wiggily.

Jimmie Wibblewobble, the duck boy, wades in all the puddles he can find.

The Bee is small, but he can make the Bear run.

The Wolf is not Uncle Wiggily's friend. He would like to have a rabbit for dinner.

Joie and Tommie Kat are very playful. They like to climb trees.

The Fox is almost as sly as the Weasel. He tries to catch Uncle Wiggily, but he never can.

The Bob Cat hunts small animals. He is always afraid that the other animals will laugh at his silly little tail.

The Ruffed Grouse is a fine, big bird. He is one of Uncle Wiggily's friends.

Billie Bushytail, the squirrel boy, likes to crack nuts with his sharp teeth.

Peetie and Jackie Bow Wow, two little puppy boys, like to play with the other animal children.

Mr. and Mrs. Robin come to Wood Land in the summer.

Uncle Wiggily Saves Baby Bunty

Find out what Uncle Wiggily did to save Baby Bunty.

"HAVE you seen Baby Bunty?" asked Uncle Wiggily Longears of Nurse Jane Fuzzy Wuzzy one day. The rabbit gentleman was standing on the front steps of his hollow stump bungalow where he was twinkling his pink nose. He was getting ready to start off and seek an adventure.

"No, I have not seen her," answered Nurse Jane in a squeaking voice. "I don't know where Baby Bunty is."

Baby Bunty was a little rabbit girl who lived in the woods not far from Uncle Wiggily's hollow stump bungalow. She was very fond of playing tricks on Mr. Longears.

Uncle Wiggily made his pink nose twinkle again as he laughed and said:

"Well, if Bunty hops along here and asks for me, don't tell her that I have gone to the woods, if you please, Miss Fuzzy Wuzzy."

"Why not?" asked the muskrat lady housekeeper.

"Because if you should tell her," answered the rabbit gentle-man, "Baby Bunty would hop after me, and want me to play tag. I am going to the woods to look for an adventure," and he tapped his red, white, and blue crutch on a stone. The crutch was striped like a barber's pole, and had been gnawed out of a cornstalk by the muskrat lady.

"Very well. If I see Baby Bunty, I shall not tell her where you have gone," promised Nurse Jane, creeping into the bungalow to do her dusting.

Away hopped Mr. Longears to the woods where lived the Fox, the Wolf, the Bear, the Bob Cat, and the Weasel. All these animals liked to catch rabbits, and they would have been very glad to catch Uncle Wiggily. He would make a fine meal, they thought.

Of all the animals, the Weasel was the most sly, and the rabbit gentleman knew this. Although the Weasel was sly and very small, he was brave and not afraid to fight animals larger than himself.

"I am not so strong as the Fox," the Weasel would whisper, "but I am more clever. The Fox and the Wolf run out into the open fields and try to catch rabbits. I will hide in a hole, beneath a stone or bush, and catch Mr. Longears that way. I will play a trick on him."

To play his sly trick and catch Uncle Wiggily, the Weasel
looked for a hole in the ground. He soon found what he wanted.
Perhaps some rabbit had dug the hole for his home.

"I shall catch Uncle Wiggily in this hole," the Weasel said.
"It is just right for a trap."

In a field, near by, grew some yellow carrots. The Weasel knew,
from having watched them eating, that rabbits were very fond of
yellow carrots.

Creeping into the field, the sly Weasel dug up a carrot that
was the color of shining copper. Taking this to the hole, the
Weasel first scattered some pieces of the carrot on the ground
outside and then threw a big slice halfway down the hole where
it could easily be seen.

"Now," whispered the Weasel to himself, "I shall hide in the
bushes near this hole. When Uncle Wiggily hops along, he will
see and smell the pieces of carrot on the ground. He will think
the hole is filled with more pieces of carrot."

"Down into the hole Uncle Wiggily will go," thought the
Weasel with a silent little laugh, "but when he is in, he can't
get out easily. Then down after him into the hole I shall glide.
In that way I shall catch a fine, big rabbit for my dinner!"

The Weasel licked his white teeth with his red tongue and smiled. Such animals love to boast of what they can do. When he had his rabbit trap all ready, the Weasel hid in the bushes and waited. He waited and waited and waited until he heard someone coming along a path through the woods.

"Here comes Uncle Wiggily!" thought the sly one, curling up into a tight ball of fur so that he might not be seen. "I shall soon have a fine dinner. Here comes Uncle Wiggily!"

But it was Baby Bunty, and not the rabbit gentleman, who came hopping along. The little rabbit girl had first gone to the hollow stump bungalow to look for Uncle Wiggily, but the rabbit gentleman was not there.

"And I am not allowed to tell you where he has gone," Nurse Jane had said.

"I can guess where he is!" shouted Baby Bunty with a laugh. "Uncle Wiggily has hopped to the woods, as he often does, to look for an adventure. I shall hop after him. He may play tag with me."

Baby Bunty hopped along to the woods. It did not take her more than a few minutes to get there. Near the edge of the woods she saw a hole in the ground with bits of carrot scattered near it. Clapping her paws, the little rabbit girl cried:

"Oh, how wonderful! What lovely yellow carrots! I am always so hungry for them!"

She quickly ate the pieces that lay on the ground outside the hole. Then, peeping into the hole, Baby Bunty saw the big, yellow slice.

"I am going down into this hole and get a lot of carrots!" happily cried the little rabbit. So into the hole poor Baby Bunty crawled.

"Ah, ha!" whispered the Weasel, hiding in the bushes. "Ah, ha! One rabbit is as good as another to me. If I cannot catch Uncle Wiggily, I shall eat Baby Bunty!"

He waited to make sure his trick would work. As soon as the little rabbit girl was out of sight, the Weasel came out of the bushes and started after her.

By this time Baby Bunty had found out that there was only one piece of carrot in the hole. As soon as she had eaten it, she turned to go out. Then she saw that the Weasel was coming toward the doorway.

"Oh!" she screamed. And again, "Oh!"

"Don't be frightened, my dear!" growled the sly Weasel. "Don't be frightened!"

But Baby Bunty was frightened. She turned quickly and tried to run out the other way, but the hole was tightly closed at that end.

"Oh, what shall I do?" thought the poor little rabbit girl. "Uncle Wiggily often told me never to go in a hole unless I saw a way to get out. I wish I had remembered what he told me. There is no way out except by the door where the Weasel is. I must try to dig another hole at the far end. I cannot hop back past the Weasel."

Then Baby Bunty, with her little paws, began to dig another door out of the hole in the ground. She dug as fast as she could, scratching the earth with her front paws and scattering it behind her with her back paws. Now and then she would turn her head, hoping the Weasel had gone. But no! There he was, creeping slowly toward her. He was inside the hole now, and he stopped for a minute now and then to rub his hungry red tongue over his hungry white teeth.

"Oh, he is surely going to get me!" thought poor Bunty, for she could see that it was going to take a long time for her to dig another door out of the hole.

Just then, on the ground up above the hole, Uncle Wiggily came hopping along. He sniffed and he snuffed and he smelled the Weasel. Then, with his long ears, the rabbit uncle heard Baby Bunty saying:

"Oh, dear! Oh, dear! Oh, dear!"

The brave old rabbit gentleman sat up straight.

"Baby Bunty is down there — in a hole — in a trap! I must dig another hole and help her out!" cried Uncle Wiggily. "I must dig fast!" Quickly, with his strong paws, Mr. Longears began digging down into the hole-trap.

Out and away flew the dirt, scattered by Uncle Wiggily's paws. Soon he had made an opening on top of the ground, and through this opening he could look down into the hole and see the small rabbit and the Weasel creeping nearer, nearer, and nearer to her.

"Quick, Baby Bunty! Up this way!" cried Mr. Longears. "I will save you! Jump up here!"

Baby Bunty, her heart beating very fast, looked up and saw Uncle Wiggily.

"Oh, how glad I am that you came!" she said.

Up through the hole which the rabbit gentleman had dug, Baby Bunty sprang. Behind her leaped the Weasel snapping his hungry teeth. But the Weasel's teeth did not bite Bunty.

"Wait! Wait!" howled the sly Weasel. "Wait a minute!"

"Thank you, we haven't time to wait!" said Uncle Wiggily.

Then, holding Baby Bunty by the paw, and before the Weasel had time to scramble up out of the hole, Mr. Longears hopped off with the little rabbit girl. They hurried through the woods and safe home to the hollow stump bungalow.

The Weasel knew he could not run fast enough to catch the two rabbits. The sly one sat looking down into the empty hole.

"Uncle Wiggily is smarter than I thought he was," growled the Weasel. "So is Baby Bunty."

Uncle Wiggily's Umbrella

Find out how Uncle Wiggily went home from the high hill.

NURSE Jane Fuzzy Wuzzy opened the door of Uncle Wiggily's hollow stump bungalow and looked out. She sniffed the air slowly and carefully.

"We shall have rain soon," spoke Nurse Jane in her squeaking voice, as she shook some dust from the feathers she had tied on the end of her long tail so that she could clean the furniture. "We shall have rain. I can smell it coming!"

"Then I had better take my umbrella with me," said Mr. Longears. "I do not want to get wet, so I had better take my umbrella."

Each day the rabbit gentleman hopped away from his bungalow, leaping across the fields, bounding through the woods, jumping over the brooks. In this way Uncle Wiggily had fun, and almost every day he found adventures.

"Adventures," Mr. Longears would explain when Uncle Butter, the goat, asked what he meant, "adventures are things that happen to you."

"It happened that I fell down today and bumped one of my horns!" bleated Uncle Butter.

"That was one kind of adventure, but not a nice kind," said the rabbit gentleman.

But this adventure had happened to the goat the day before Nurse Jane smelled the rain coming.

"I hope I may have an adventure with my umbrella this afternoon," said the rabbit gentleman as he hopped down his bungalow steps. "We have had no rain for a long time, so I have not carried my umbrella."

"You may have two adventures," squeaked Miss Fuzzy Wuzzy turning to go inside to finish her housework. "The wind is beginning to blow very hard, as it always blows before a rain storm. If you don't watch out, the wind may blow your umbrella away, and then you will get all wet. That would make two adventures, I think."

"You are right!" laughed the rabbit uncle, "but they would be sad adventures. I do not so much mind getting wet myself, if the rain will not spot my red, white, and blue striped crutch that you gnawed for me out of a cornstalk. However, I shall not need my crutch today, because I have no pains in my legs. I will take my umbrella."

Nurse Jane reached one paw into the stand near the front bungalow door, took out his umbrella, and gave it to Uncle Wiggily. He thanked her and then, with a twinkle on the end of his pink nose, he looked at the muskrat lady housekeeper.

"Do you wish to see me do a trick with this umbrella?" asked Mr. Longears.

"What trick can you do with it?" Miss Fuzzy Wuzzy at once wanted to know.

"I can put this umbrella up and down at the same time," answered the rabbit.

"Let me see you do it," begged Nurse Jane. She was very fond of tricks.

Uncle Wiggily opened his umbrella with a strong push, holding it over his head as if it were raining.

"Now it is up!" he cried with a jolly laugh.

"Yes," answered Nurse Jane, "now it is up. I can see that. But it is not down at the same time and you said it would be."

While the umbrella was still up, or open, Uncle Wiggily quickly put it down on the floor of the porch, with the handle up in the air.

"Now my umbrella is down!" he cried. "It is also up! It is up and down at the same time! Ha! Ha!"

Nurse Jane also laughed, "Ha! Ha!" She laughed so hard that some of the feathers she had tied on the end of her tail to make a duster were shaken loose.

"Yes! Yes!" said the muskrat lady. "I see! Now your umbrella is down, and at the same time it is up! That was a good trick! Can you do any more?"

"I have no time to do more tricks," answered the rabbit. "I must go look for an adventure."

Nurse Jane was still laughing.

"Uncle Wiggily's umbrella can be up when it is down, and down when it is up," said the muskrat lady watching the rabbit close his opened umbrella and lay it down on the porch. "It is very funny. If he opened his umbrella down in the cellar, it would be up and down at the same time. But if he put it down when he was up in the attic — Oh, dear! Oh, dear!" laughed Miss Fuzzy Wuzzy, "I must not go on in this way or I shall become a player of tricks like Uncle Wiggily. I must stop playing and bake a carrot pie."

"I shall eat some of that carrot pie when I come back from my adventure," said Uncle Wiggily. "Now I shall take up my umbrella that was down," and the rabbit gentleman still had a joking look on his face. "I shall take my umbrella and hop away."

Down the gravel walk in front of his bungalow the bunny gentleman hopped, and on through the woods where the wind was blowing hard. Mr. Longears saw black clouds gathering in the west.

"It will rain soon," said Uncle Wiggily, speaking aloud.

"And I shall eat soon!" cried a voice.

"Ha! That must have been an echo!" whispered Mr. Longears. It must have been an echo. I always thought an echo gave you back the same words that you spoke, but this echo was different."

He looked around but could see no one. Of course he knew he could not see an echo. It can only be heard.

"It will rain soon," said Uncle Wiggily again.

"And I shall eat soon!" cried the other voice.

"It must be an echo!" said the rabbit.

"I am not an echo!" called the voice.

"Who are you, then?" asked Mr. Longears in surprise.

"I am the Hungry Hawk!" was the answer.

"The Hungry Hawk!" cried Uncle Wiggily. He was beginning to feel a little bit afraid now. "The Hungry Hawk! Oh, dear me!"

Down out of a tree swooped a big bird. He was a hawk, and hawks are always hungry. This hawk bird had sharp claws, a sharp beak, and strong wings. Swooping down on his wings out of the air, the Hawk, with his sharp claws and sharp beak, could catch rabbits to eat when he was hungry. It seems too bad that this is so, but it is.

"I am going to catch you and eat you, Uncle Wiggily!" cried the Hawk in a hoarse, croaking voice. "I am hungry and I must have a rabbit to eat!"

"Could you not eat something else?" asked the rabbit politely.

"No! I must have you!" snapped the Hawk, clashing his sharp beak.

Faster and faster down through the air he flew until the wind whistled under his spread-out wings, and his feathers fluttered.

Uncle Wiggily hopped as fast as he could, but hopping seemed slower than flying.

"Wait! Wait for me!" called the Hawk. "I must get you! I must eat you!"

"No! No! You shall not get me! You shall not eat me!" cried the rabbit gentleman, bravely twinkling his pink nose. Away he hopped, faster than ever.

"Stop! Stop!" cried the big bird. "I must eat you! I am so very hungry!"

"No! No!" called back Uncle Wiggily over his shoulder as he leaped along. "I do not want to be eaten!" He held his umbrella under his left paw as he hopped.

Uncle Wiggily ran! He hopped! He leaped! He jumped this way and he jumped that way! But the Hawk flew after him faster than before. Only the tangled grapevines, under which the rabbit slipped now and then, saved him from being caught at once. Once a number of strawberry vines held one of Uncle Wiggily's paws and he stumbled, falling down. But he shook himself loose and was up and running on again before the Hawk could catch him. The big bird, however, was flying nearer, nearer, and nearer all the while.

Quite out of breath, at last Uncle Wiggily reached the edge of a high hill. It was at the end of a path near the edge of the woods. The hill was very steep, and, as he hopped toward it, the rabbit looked up at the sky hoping it might start to rain.

"If it would only rain," thought Uncle Wiggily, "water might splash into the eyes of the Hawk. Then he could not see to catch me."

The wind was blowing and the clouds were black, but no rain fell from the sky. And still the Hawk was flying on after the rabbit gentleman.

Mr. Longears was now at the upper edge of the high hill. It was very steep and it was a long way to the ground below at the foot of the hill. Uncle Wiggily could see his hollow stump bungalow, nestling under the trees. In the doorway stood Nurse Jane with her broom.

"If Miss Fuzzy Wuzzy would only look up here, she might shake her broom at the Hawk and frighten him away," thought Uncle Wiggily as he heard the rushing wings of the big bird coming nearer. "But she does not know I am up here. If it were not so far down to the bottom of this steep hill, I might jump. Then the Hawk could not catch me, because I could run into my bungalow. I dare not jump! Oh, what shall I do?"

Nearer and nearer came the Hawk, crying, "I am going to get you! I am very hungry for a fat rabbit!"

Suddenly the wind began to blow harder. The rain came pelting down in splashy drops. Uncle Wiggily stood on the edge of the steep hill and raised his umbrella to keep off the rain.

"I am coming! I am coming!" cried the Hawk, shaking himself loose where he had become tangled in a grapevine that hung from the branches of a tree. "I am coming!"

The strong wind pulled and tugged at the rabbit's open umbrella. All at once the wind puffed itself up and under the black cloth, stretching and creaking the steel ribs.

"Oh, the wind is trying to blow away my umbrella!" cried Uncle Wiggily. With all his might he clung to the handle.

"Whish! Swish! Swosh!" The wind blew Uncle Wiggily and his umbrella clear off the top of the high, steep hill just before the Hawk reached the spot.

"Oh, I am falling down!" shouted the rabbit in alarm.

His umbrella was up and open. Under it the wind puffed itself, and the umbrella held Uncle Wiggily up just as a large toy balloon might have done, or as if he had a white parachute, such as men use when they leap from airplanes.

Very gently, as he clung to the open umbrella, Uncle Wiggily floated down toward the ground below. Down, down, down, softly the rabbit gentleman floated until he had landed safely on the grass in front of his hollow stump bungalow.

The Hawk, fierce and hungry as he was, dared not fly down there to get the rabbit, for the big bird was afraid of Nurse Jane and her broomstick. Hawks hate broomsticks.

"Ho! Ho!" joyfully squeaked the muskrat lady as she stood in the doorway of the hollow stump bungalow and saw the rabbit gentleman float gently down. "Ho! Ho! You came in an airship, didn't you, Uncle Wiggily? That, surely, was an adventure!"

"Yes," answered the rabbit, "you might say that my umbrella turned into an airship to save me from the Hawk. I always felt sure my umbrella would be of some other use to me than keeping off the rain."

He laughed and patted the handle of the umbrella.

Angry at the trick the wind had played on him, the Hawk flew back through the rain to his nest in the high tree. He did not hear the tune the wind tried to whistle on his broad wings, nor did he feel his feathers flutter.

The Hawk was still very hungry. But Uncle Wiggily was home safe in his hollow stump bungalow.

Nannie Washes the Dishes

Find out how many dishes were broken.

ONE DAY, as Uncle Wiggily was hopping past the house in the woods where Nannie Wagtail lived, the rabbit gentleman heard the little goat girl bleating loudly and saying:

"Oh, I don't want to wash the supper dishes! I don't like to wash dishes!"

"Neither do I like washing dishes, Nannie," bleated Mrs. Wagtail, the lady goat. "But I have washed them for this family a great many years. Very often I get tired of washing dishes, and I think it is not too much to ask you to wash and dry them just this once."

The rabbit listened, and soon he heard Nannie say:

"Oh, I'm sorry, Mother! I wish I hadn't spoken so quickly. I'm going to wash the dishes for you!"

"I thought you would," answered Mrs. Wagtail in a low voice.

Mr. Longears liked Nannie, and he was glad to hear her say she would help her mother. After waiting a minute or two, Uncle Wiggily hopped into the house of the goat family. He often called to pay short visits.

"You are just in time, Mr. Longears!" bleated Mrs. Wagtail. "Uncle Butter and I are going to see the moving pictures, and you must come with us. Nannie is going to stay in and wash the dishes."

"That is very kind of Nannie," said the rabbit gentleman. "But I think I shall not go to the movies with you, if you please, Mrs. Wagtail, though I thank you for asking me. I shall stay here with Nannie and watch her giving the cups and saucers their evening bath!"

"Oh, now you are joking!" said Nannie, laughing. "Dishes don't take baths!"

"They do when you give them baths," answered Mr. Longears. "Where is your brother Billie?" he asked, for he did not see the boy goat prancing around.

"Billie is out playing marbles with Jackie and Peetie Bow Wow," spoke Mrs. Wagtail.

"Well, then he cannot watch Nannie giving the dishes their evening bath!" said Uncle Wiggily, and Nannie laughed again.

She no longer felt so cross at having to stay in and wash the plates, knives, and forks.

"I suppose Nannie loves to do housework, doesn't she?" asked Mr. Longears while Mrs. Wagtail was waiting for Uncle Butter,

the goat gentleman, to prance along with her to the moving pictures.

"Well, I would not exactly say that," slowly answered the goat lady, looking a little sad.

Nannie suddenly stamped her front feet and shook her horns.

"I don't like housework and I never will!" she bleated. "And I just hate doing the dishes! But I couldn't be happy, if I didn't take my turn, when I know how many times Mother has washed them."

"At least it is kind of you to feel that way about your mother, my dear," said Uncle Wiggily to Nannie.

"Oh, Nannie doesn't mean all she says when she talks about not liking to wash the dishes," bleated Uncle Butter, as he tapped with his horns on the front steps to let Mrs. Wagtail know he was ready to go to the movies. "Nannie is a good little goat!"

"I suppose, after all, it isn't much fun to wash dishes," said Uncle Wiggily, as the two goats pranced off to see the pictures. "Still Nannie, we must all do our share of work in this world, you know."

"Oh, yes, I guess so!" said Nannie. "All the same, I like to go to the movies better than I like washing dishes."

Uncle Wiggily laughed as he twinkled his pink nose just a little on one side, and he said:

"I am going to help you, Nannie! Let me make the soap suds. We shall wash the dishes together. It will not take long, and it will be fun!"

"So it will!" said Nannie. Really, she was feeling quite happy now.

The rabbit gentleman splashed the cake of soap in the hot water and soon had the tin pan filled with soapy bubbles. The bubbles glowed and glistened like a thousand dewdrops off the the end of the rainbow.

"Put the dishes in the water, Nannie," said Uncle Wiggily, and the little goat girl did as she was told.

By this time Mr. Longears had made so much soapy suds that the dishes were very slippery. When Nannie lifted out a teacup to put it in the second pan of hot, clean water, why, that teacup seemed to jump from her hoof and dart toward the floor.

"Oh, please don't break!" bleated Nannie, as she tried to catch the falling cup in the folds of her dress. "Please don't break!"

The cup would have struck the floor and it would have broken but for Uncle Wiggily. The rabbit gentleman was very quick and spry. Oh, he was very spry. He leaped over a chair, put out his paw, and with it caught the slippery, soapy cup as it slid past Nannie's dress. Just as the cup was about to crash to the floor, Uncle Wiggily caught it.

"Oh!" gasped Nannie, and her heart was beating very fast. "Oh! Thank you, Uncle Wiggily! That was Daddy's coffee cup. I don't know what I should have done if it had broken."

"Well, it didn't!" laughed the rabbit, as he put the cup in the clean, hot water to rinse. Dishes must be put to rinse in a second water after being washed in the first, soapy one.

Next Nannie lifted a large plate out of the suds, and it, also, was so slippery, from too much soap on it, that it slipped away from the little goat girl.

"Oh, please, plate, don't break!" bleated Nannie. "Please don't!"

Again Mr. Longears was very quick and spry. This time he jumped over a stool and caught the plate before it could fall to the floor and crack into a dozen pieces.

"Thank you twice!" bleated Nannie.

"We must be more careful, my dear!" Uncle Wiggily told her. He was a little out of breath from his two quick jumps.

When the plate had been put in the hot water to rinse, the little goat girl reached down into the pan of suds to pick out a large, heavy dish that had held potatoes for supper. Just as Nannie lifted up this dish, all covered with slippery soap suds, the back door suddenly opened. In bounced the Wolf.

"Gurr! Gurr! Gurr!" growled the Wolf. "Gurr! Gurr! Gurr!"

"What do you want here? How dare you come in?" shouted Uncle Wiggily, bravely twinkling his pink nose. "This is no place for you, Mr. Wolf. It isn't your den. Please get out!"

The rabbit gentleman tried to be polite, even to a Wolf.

"Well do I know this isn't my den!" the Wolf howled. "But you are here, Uncle Wiggily, and I came to get you!" Most hungrily he looked at the rabbit.

"Oh! Oh, dear! Oh, dear me!" cried Nannie. "Oh, this is awful! Oh, dear me!"

She now had lifted the heavy potato dish from the pan so that the suds and water from it dripped on the kitchen floor. The dish was so heavy that Nannie trembled as she tried to hold it.

"Oh, it's slipping! It's slipping!" cried the little goat girl. "It's going to fall and smash!"

"What is going to fall and smash?" asked the Wolf with a growl.

Before Nannie could answer there sounded in the kitchen a sudden BANG!

The heavy potato dish fell right on the hind paws of the Wolf, as he crouched to spring at the rabbit gentleman. This time the dish was really broken.

"Oh! Ouch!" howled the Wolf. "Ouchee!" He jumped high in the air, trying to shake the sharp pieces of the broken dish off his paws.

"Ouch!" howled the Wolf for the third time. "Oh, my paws! My sore paws! I'm going home! I'm going home and jump into bed. I need a doctor!"

Limping on three legs, for one had quite a long cut in it from the broken dish, the Wolf ran away, using his red tongue to soothe his sore paw.

"I am glad I stayed home to wash the dishes," bleated Nannie, when the rabbit gentleman had locked the door so that the Wolf could not come in again. "We had a great adventure, didn't we, Uncle Wiggily?" asked Nannie shyly.

"Indeed we did!" laughed the rabbit gentleman. "Tomorrow I hope I have another."

"Maybe I'll have one, too," said Nannie.

Uncle Wiggily and the Sad Rock

Find out why the little stones would not talk to the Sad Rock.

HIGH up on the side of a long hill, not far from Uncle Wiggily's hollow stump bungalow, a great rock stood out of the rough ground. The rock was almost as large as the bungalow in which the rabbit gentleman lived. The hollow stump stood in the middle of a green, grassy place, with soft, clinging vines growing about it, but the rock thrust itself out of the earth all alone.

Uncle Wiggily often liked to jump up on top of the big rock to look around. From the top the rabbit could see all over the pretty little valley below him — a valley where he had lived for many years in his hollow stump bungalow.

Mr. Longears was standing on the rock one day when he heard a sigh. It was as if someone had said: "Oh, dear!"

Uncle Wiggily gasped. "What's that? Can there be anyone under this heavy rock?" The rabbit looked over the edge, but he could see no one. Then again the voice sighed:

"Oh, dear!"

"There must be someone here!" said the rabbit, "yet I can see no one."

Then he called in a louder voice. "Who is saying 'Oh, dear?' Tell me!"

"I am!" answered the voice, and it came right from under Uncle Wiggily's paws, making him jump in surprise. "I was saying, 'Oh, dear!' if you please — I, the Sad Rock."

"Do you mean to tell me that you spoke just now?" asked the rabbit.

"I did," answered the Rock. And then Uncle Wiggily saw that the Rock had a face. True, it was a face made only of patches of green moss clinging to the rock, but still it was a face, with eyes, ears, a nose, and a mouth. It was not a happy face.

"I spoke," sighed the Rock. "I wonder if you cannot help me? I am very sad! I am the Sad Rock!"

"My! My! This is most surprising!" said the Rabbit. "In the first place, I never knew before that a rock could talk. In the second place, how can I help you? And in the third place, why are you the Sad Rock?"

"Because I am so much alone," the Rock answered. "Up on this hillside I have very little company. There are no trees near me to whisper secrets. I am so large that the birds seem afraid to perch on me to rest. They may think I am a trap. And because I am so big, none of the little rocks around here will talk to me. They think I am proud of my size, I suppose, but I am not."

The Rock sighed.

"A sad and lonely rock," said Uncle Wiggily softly. "This is too bad! I will help you if I can. What do you want me to do?"

"I wish you would stop and talk to me each day as you hop past," answered the Rock. "I often watch you going to seek adventures, but you seldom stop. You are always in a hurry. Today I made up my mind that I would speak to you and ask you to cure me of being sad."

"I shall be glad to do what I can," said the rabbit gentleman politely. "How shall I begin?"

"Tell me of your adventures," begged the Rock, and now the face of green moss was less sad. It seemed to smile a little as a sunbeam tickled it.

"I have had no adventures yet today," answered Uncle Wiggily. "I was just hopping along to look for one when I heard your voice. But I can tell you of an adventure I had yesterday."

"Please do," begged the Rock.

Uncle Wiggily then told how he had helped Nannie Wagtail to wash the dishes, and how the soapy potato dish had slipped, fallen, and cut the paw of the bad Wolf.

"Ha! Ha!" laughed the Rock when the tale was finished. "That was a good adventure story! Ho! Ho! I should like to have seen that Wolf limping back to his den. If I had been there, I would have tried to roll on his tail to pinch it."

"You do not look as sad as you did at first," said Uncle Wiggily. "You are quite cheerful." And again he looked at the mossy face, which was now smiling at him.

"No, I am not so sad, now," the Rock answered. "But please tell me another adventure story. You have done me so much good. I shall not mind so much, now, staying here all alone, without even a tree to whisper to me. Though I shall miss the birds who perch on other stones, but never on me, I shall be happy when I think of you, Uncle Wiggily. You have been so kind."

"I am glad of that," spoke the rabbit. "It is very easy to be kind."

"I wish the little rocks near me would talk to me," the big Rock went on, "but I shall not mind so much, now, if they do not. I shall think of how Nannie dropped the dish on the paw of the Wolf. That was funny!"

"Yes, it was funny, Mr. Rock," said Mr. Longears. He was glad to see the Rock more cheerful.

"Please tell me another story," again begged the Rock. "I can think of them when I am up here all alone."

The rabbit said he was sorry but he could not do that. He had no more time just then.

"I must seek a new adventure," said Uncle Wiggily. "When I find one, I will come back and tell you," he promised the Rock. "Each day after this I shall stop and speak to you."

"Then I shall no longer be lonely or sad," the Rock said, and his big, mossy face wrinkled in a most jolly way as the sun shone on it.

Uncle Wiggily hopped away, down the hill, over the fields, and through the woods.

Adventures were scarce, but he had to make a boat out of a large grapevine leaf so a little red Ant Lady could sail across the brook. When she was safe on the other side of the water, the Ant Lady

crawled out of her leaf-boat. She blew a kiss to Uncle Wiggily and thanked him. Then she hurried on her way. Ants always seem to be in a great hurry.

"That was hardly enough of an adventure for me to tell to the Rock," thought Uncle Wiggily, as he hopped back toward his home in the hollow stump bungalow. "I shall wait until tomorrow to go and see him. Then I may have another tale to tell."

It was late in the day and getting dark when the rabbit gentleman hopped along the path in Wood Land where he lived. As he passed the Knot Hole House, where Mr. and Mrs. Longtail, the mice, had their home, Uncle Wiggily heard Jollie and Jillie, the mouse children, talking.

"We can't find her anywhere," one said.

"Have you looked in the fields?" squeaked Mrs. Longtail.

"Yes, Mother," answered Jillie. "We have looked and looked all through the fields!"

"Have you looked in the woods?" squeaked Mr. Longtail.

"Yes, Daddy," answered Jollie. "We have looked and looked all through the woods, too!"

"But we can't find her anywhere!" squeaked Jollie and Jillie together, just like twins, though Jollie was really older than his sister.

"Ha!" said Uncle Wiggily to himself. "Someone must be lost! I wonder who it can be? Perhaps I can help find whoever it is."

Hopping to the door of the Knot Hole House, where the mouse family lived, Uncle Wiggily made a low and polite bow as he raised his tall silk hat off his head.

"May I have the pleasure of helping you?" he asked.

"Oh, Uncle Wiggily!" squeaked Jollie and Jillie in delight at seeing the rabbit gentleman. "You are just the one we were wishing for!"

"What is the matter?" asked Mr. Longears, smoothing down his silk hat with the end of his pink, twinkling nose.

"Squeakie Eekie, our little cousin mouse, is lost," answered Jollie sadly.

"We can't find her anywhere!" added Jillie.

"That's too bad!" said Uncle Wiggily.

"But come with me, Jollie and Jillie," he added. "We shall soon find Squeakie Eekie. Don't you worry, Mr. and Mrs. Longtail. You stay in the Knot Hole House and have a thimbleful of warm milk ready for the cousin mouse when Jollie, Jillie, and I bring her home. We are sure to find her!"

It was growing darker, but Uncle Wiggily was not afraid in the night, nor were the two mouse children, so they hurried on after Mr. Longears. He hopped toward his bungalow.

"Where are you going?" squeaked Jollie. "Cousin mouse isn't at your house, is she?"

"No," answered the rabbit. "But I am going to get my lantern so that we can see better to search for Squeakie Eekie."

Uncle Wiggily's lantern was a bottle filled with flashing lightning bugs, and it gleamed cheerfully and pleasantly in the dark night as the rabbit hopped out of his bungalow with it. He and

Jollie and Jillie looked again in the woods and fields for Squeakie Eekie, but they could not find the cousin mouse.

Then Mr. Longears saw in front of him the long hill where the Sad Rock stood in the brown earth.

"We will look there for Squeakie Eekie," said the rabbit, "and if we do not find her, we will call the Police Dog."

When they all came near to the big Rock, they heard voices talking, and one was the voice of Squeakie Eekie!

"Do you think they will ever find me?" she was saying. "Oh, I am lost! And the night is so dark! I do not know my way back to the Knot Hole House. What shall I do?"

"Stay right here with me, little cousin mouse!" said another voice. "Nothing can harm you in the little hole you dug under my edge with your tiny paws. The rain cannot wet you, nor even the heavy dew. The Weasel will not dare come near you as long as you are near me. In the morning it will be light enough to see your way home. I will take care of you in the night, never fear!"

"That is my friend, the Sad Rock, speaking!" cried Uncle Wiggily gladly.

"Squeakie Eekie is there, too!" shouted Jollie joyfully

"Hi, Squeakie Eekie! Are you there?" called Jillie, too impatient to wait longer.

Uncle Wiggily hopped forward with his firefly lantern.

"Yes! Yes! I am here," squeaked back the cousin mouse. "Oh, I am so glad you have come for me! I went to the store to get some cheese, but I lost my way. Then I found this big stone. I dug a little nest for myself under the edge. I am so glad you found me."

"Uncle Wiggily found you," said Jollie. "He is here with us."

The fireflies in the bottle lantern raised their wings and made a brighter light by which the rabbit gentleman could see Squeakie Eekie curled up in a tiny hole in the soft earth under the shelter of the Sad Rock. Uncle Wiggily saw that the mossy face of the big stone was still smiling, so Mr. Rock could not be very sad.

"Everything is all right now," happily sighed Squeakie Eekie, creeping out to her cousins and the rabbit gentleman. "I am going home with you."

"Are you going to leave me?" asked the Rock.

"Yes," Squeakie answered. "But I want to thank you very much for giving me shelter from the dark night. I was no longer afraid when I saw how big and strong you were there above me."

If the Rock had been alive, he might have looked proud — not too proud, you understand, but just proud enough. He might have made a polite bow to the cousin mouse. But how can a rock ever make a bow? As it was, he only tried to smile more cheerfully with his mossy face.

"I am very glad I could help you, Squeakie Eekie," said the Rock. "Any time you get lost, just come to me. I will care for you."

Squeakie Eekie promised that she would, and then she hurried down the hill with Jollie and Jillie. Uncle Wiggily followed more slowly. Before the rabbit had gone very far, he heard the Rock again calling to him.

"Yes! What is it?" asked Mr. Longears.

"You are not the only one who can have adventures!" said the Rock. "I had one, too! Though I am so large that the birds seem to fear to perch on me; though there are no trees near to whisper to me; though none of the other rocks will talk to me — still I had an adventure! I am never going to be sad any more because I shall always think of how I helped Squeakie Eekie!" The Rock seemed happy at last.

"I shall often stop and tell you of my adventures," promised the rabbit gentleman as he started to hop away again. "You have many friends, now."

Then came whispers all around the big Rock, and a small red stone spoke out of the darkness.

"You will not be lonesome or sad any more, Big Rock, for we small stones will talk to you now," said the Red Stone.

"Why did you not do that before?" asked Uncle Wiggily, turning back with his firefly lantern.

"Because," answered the Red Stone, "when we looked at Big Rock, his mossy face seemed so cross that we were afraid he might roll over and crush us. His face is no longer sad. He smiles! Now he will be one of us! He might even be our uncle!"

"Yes, indeed!" said the Big Rock. "I shall gladly be an uncle to all the Little Stones."

Uncle Wiggily laughed softly as he hopped down the hill with his firefly lantern after Jollie, Jillie, and Squeakie Eekie, the cousin mouse.

Uncle Wiggily and the Bee

Baby Bunty did not think that a bee could ever help Uncle Wiggily.
Find out if she was right.

"NURSE Jane, we shall go away from here very soon," Uncle Wiggily told his muskrat lady housekeeper one morning.

"Do you mean we shall be going away from our hollow stump bungalow?" squeaked Miss Fuzzy Wuzzy in surprise.

"Yes," answered Mr. Longears, "we shall be going away soon."

"Where are we going?" Nurse Jane wanted to know.

"For a time we are going to live on a farm," said the bunny rabbit gentleman.

"Oh, I am so glad," squeaked the muskrat lady. "A farm is beautiful in summer."

"May I come with you?" suddenly asked a little voice, and into the bungalow kitchen hopped Baby Bunty. "Please take me to the farm," she begged. "I have always wanted to live on a farm. I want to see how they plant honey, and I want to watch them gather the eggs off trees."

"Ho! Ho!" laughed Uncle Wiggily. "It is easy to see, Baby Bunty, that you are too young to know much about a farm. No one plants honey."

"Well," said the little rabbit girl, "honey is sweet and so are carrots. I have seen you plant seed to make carrots grow. So I should think that honey could grow out of the ground just as carrots do."

"Honey is quite different from carrots!" said Mr. Longears. "Honey is made by bees who gather sweet juices from the flowers. The bees change the juices into honey."

"Oh, I didn't know that!" said Baby Bunty.

"And eggs are not picked off trees," added Nurse Jane. "You ought to know that, Bunty. You have gone often enough for me to the coop of Mrs. Cluck-Cluck, the hen lady. You ought to know, by this time, that hens and birds lay eggs. They are not picked off trees."

"Yes, I should have remembered that," said Bunty. "But will you please take me to the farm with you?" she begged Uncle Wiggily. "I should love to see the bees gathering honey."

"I will think about it," was all Mr. Longears would promise.

"If you take her," whispered Nurse Jane, while Bunty was looking in the pantry to see if there might be a piece of carrot pie on the shelf, "if you take Bunty, Mr. Longears, she may play tricks on you."

"Oh, a few tricks will do me good, I think!" answered the bunny rabbit. "So we will take Baby Bunty to the farm with us."

"Oh, goodie! goodie! goodie!" cried the little rabbit girl, clapping her paws. She had heard what was said. Then she ran off to tell her friends the good news.

The next day Uncle Wiggily, Nurse Jane, and Baby Bunty traveled to the farm, about two miles away from the hollow stump bungalow.

There were broad fields and wide green meadows at the farm. In the meadows the sheep ate the grass, and in the fields the cows chewed the sweet clover leaves.

Uncle Wiggily saw one brown cow which ate green clover. The green clover was turned into white milk, and out of the white milk and cream was churned yellow butter.

"My name is Mrs. Moo," the cow told Baby Bunty.

"I wish you would tell me how you churn butter," begged the little rabbit girl of the cow.

"I do not churn it," answered Mrs. Moo. "The farmer's wife does that. She pours milk and cream into a barrel and beats it up and down with a long stick. Soon lumps of yellow butter appear in the barrel with the milk. That is called churning."

"It is quite like a magic trick, isn't it?" laughed Bunty.

"Quite like a trick, indeed," said Uncle Wiggily. "But you must not play any tricks on me while we are at the farm, Bunty!"

He said that just in time to stop her from tickling his pink nose with a long stem of green grass.

Baby Bunty laughed. So did the rabbit gentleman. It is quite jolly even to think of a funny trick.

That afternoon Uncle Wiggily, Nurse Jane, and Baby Bunty traveled across a field of the farm, toward the birch woods. Near a stone wall in a damp meadow they saw some flowers growing.

"Oh, see the lovely blossoms!" squeaked Miss Fuzzy Wuzzy.

"I'm going to pick some!" cried Baby Bunty. But when she went to pick one of the flowers, she jumped back as if afraid.

"What is the matter?" asked Uncle Wiggily.

"There is a bug on the flower plant," answered Bunty.

Uncle Wiggily hopped close to look, and he laughed as he said:

"That is only a honey-bug, Baby Bunty. It is a honey-bug, a bee, and it will not bite you or sting you if you do not harm it."

"Oh, I wouldn't harm it!" said Bunty, quickly. She did not go close to the flower again.

"I could not sting anyone now if I wanted to," buzzed the Bee. "Not that I would ever sting Bunty. I am in much trouble! I wish someone would help me!"

"What is the trouble?" Uncle Wiggily wanted to know. "I will help you if I can."

"The trouble is that I am caught fast on this plant," buzzed the honey Bee. "I flew on it to get some of the sweet juice, but, all of a sudden, I found myself held fast by my legs. I cannot get loose to fly back to the hive to make honey from the juice."

"Let me see what is the matter," said the rabbit gentleman as he leaned closer over the bee. Then he said, "Ah, my little buzzing friend, your legs are caught in a pitcher plant."

"What is a pitcher plant?" asked Baby Bunty.

"It is a plant that catches flies," answered the rabbit gentleman.

"This plant gives off a sweet smell. When flies alight on it, they are caught in a trap which the plant has ready to hold them."

"I should have known better than to try to get honey from this pitcher plant," buzzed the Bee.

"We all make mistakes," said Uncle Wiggily. "Now I will help you."

Gently he loosened the legs of the bee so that the honey-bug could fly away.

"Thank you, Mr. Longears!" buzzed the Bee. "You have done me a great favor, and some day I hope I may be able to do one for you."

"Ho! Ho!" laughed Baby Bunty. "How can a little bee ever do a favor for a big rabbit?"

"Hush, Bunty! That isn't polite!" whispered the rabbit gentleman. "You never can tell what is going to happen in this world."

Up in the air, off Uncle Wiggily's paw, flew the Bee. It was glad to be free again. On toward the hive it flew, calling back thanks to Uncle Wiggily.

The next day, when Uncle Wiggily, Nurse Jane, and Baby Bunty were again wandering about the farm, they found a little grassy hollow where spice bushes grew.

"What a lovely place for a party," said Baby Bunty. She was just going to pull up a grass stem, and once more try to tickle Uncle Wiggily on the end of his pink, twinkling nose, when the rabbit gentleman suddenly whispered:

"What's that?"

There was a noise behind the spice bush.

"Gurr! Gurr! Gurr!" came a loud growl. "I smell honey! I smell rabbits! I smell a muskrat!" A big, black bear rushed out from behind the spice bush.

Uncle Wiggily, Nurse Jane, and Baby Bunty tried to run, but their feet were tangled in the thick grass. Before they could go very far the Bear caught up to them.

"Gurr! Gurr! Gurr!" he growled again. "I smell honey! I smell Uncle Wiggily! I am going to eat Uncle Wiggily! Then I shall eat you, little rabbit girl!" He looked straight at Baby Bunty.

"Oh! Oh, dear!" the little rabbit girl cried, trying to hide behind Nurse Jane.

"And then," went on the Bear, "I shall eat Miss Fuzzy Wuzzy. And then I shall eat some honey!" The Bear rolled his tongue over his sharp teeth. "Oh, what a fine meal I am going to have!"

Nurse Jane looked for a stone to throw at the Bear. Baby Bunty looked for a hollow log in which to hide. Uncle Wiggily looked to see if the Police Dog might not be coming, but there was no sign of him.

A moment later the big Bear made a jump for Mr. Longears, but at that very moment a loud buzzing noise sounded in the air above, and along flew a hundred bees. They were led by the Bee which Uncle Wiggily, the day before, had set free from the sticky flower.

"What is all this?" growled the Bear. Oh, he had a very loud growl. "What is all this? No wonder I smelled honey, with so many bees flying around! But what do you bees want?" asked the Bear.

"We want you to let Uncle Wiggily alone," answered the Bee leader — the Bee that Uncle Wiggily had helped. "We want you to go back to your den. You must not eat either of these rabbits or Nurse Jane!"

"Who can stop me?" growled the Bear. He was trying to untangle his paws from the long grass that had caught them as it had caught the paws of Uncle Wiggily and the others. "Who can stop me?"

"We shall stop you!" buzzed the Bee leader. "Ho, my friends!" the leader called to the other honey-bugs. "Drive away this growling Bear!"

"We shall drive him away!" hummed the other bees.

Flying down at the big Bear, they stung him on his soft and tender nose, on his ears and around his eyes, where he had no thick fur to cover him. Oh, how the bees stung that Bear!

"Wuff! Wuff!" he howled in pain and anger, pawing at his face to drive away the bees. "I'll be good! Wuff! Wuff! I won't bite Uncle Wiggily! I won't bite Nurse Jane. I won't bite the little rabbit girl! And I won't take any honey! Let me go!"

Then, with some of the bees still buzzing around him, away ran the Bear, as fast as he could run, crying:

"Wuff! Wuff! Wuff!"

"Oh, isn't it wonderful!" laughed Baby Bunty, as she danced around the rabbit gentleman and Nurse Jane. "The Bee did you a favor after all, didn't he, Uncle Wiggily?"

"Yes," answered the bunny rabbit. "One does not need to be big and strong to do favors, Bunty. But how did you know I was in trouble?" asked Mr. Longears of the Bee.

"I was flying along with my friends when I looked down and saw the Bear trying to get you," was the answer. "And now we must hurry to our honey-making," buzzed the Bee. "The hive must be filled. Now that we have driven away the Bear, we must be busy little bees and gather honey."

"Good-by!" called Baby Bunty, waving her paw to the honey-bugs. As they flew out of sight, she and Uncle Wiggily and Nurse Jane hopped back to the farmhouse.

Uncle Wiggily Catches the Bear

Find out who did not get any pie.

"UNCLE WIGGILY! Oh, ho, Uncle Wiggily!" called Nurse Jane one morning as she crept around the kitchen of the farmhouse. She had just finished washing the dishes. "Ho! Where are you, Uncle Wiggily?" the muskrat lady squeaked.

"Here I am. What do you want?" answered Mr. Longears as he hopped in off the side porch where he had been warming his pink nose in the sunshine. "What is it, Nurse Jane?"

"If you will hop around to an apple tree, and bring me some apples, I will make you a pie," promised Miss Fuzzy Wuzzy.

"Oh, that will be fun!" said the bunny rabbit gentleman. "I shall hop around as fast as I can to look for apples. I am very fond of pie."

Many trees grew on the farm. Some trees had peaches on their branches. On other trees grew plums. There were pears on the trees at the south end of the farm. At the north end stood one tree on which hung apples with round, red cheeks.

Hopping here and hopping there, at last Uncle Wiggily reached the apple tree. But, alas! Although the branches were thick with the red fruit, the apples grew so high up that the bunny rabbit could not reach them, even by standing on his tiptoes. He looked around, but he could find no apples on the ground. Perhaps some boys had picked up those that had fallen.

"Maybe if I shook the tree, I could make some apples fall down," thought Uncle Wiggily. He tried, but of course he was not strong enough to shake the tree; so no apples fell.

"If the wind would only blow hard enough, it would shake loose some apples," thought Mr. Longears. But the wind blew very gently, hardly enough to stir the green leaves.

"If I could throw a stone up into the tree, I might hit some apples and knock them down," said Uncle Wiggily. He was beginning to think he would get no apples for Nurse Jane's pie. He tried once more. Up into the tree he threw stone after stone, but none was large enough to knock down even a small apple.

"Dear me! How am I ever going to get any apples for Nurse Jane to bake in a pie?" thought the rabbit. He wanted that pie very much.

Suddenly there was a noise in the bushes near the tree. Mr. Longears thought the Fox, the Wolf, the Bob Cat, or the Weasel was coming to get him. Then out of the bushes walked Tommie and Joie Kat. The two pussy boys walked in the grass with their tails held high and stiff in the air like fishing poles.

"Hello, Tommie and Joie!" Uncle Wiggily called to the pussy boys. The rabbit gentleman was glad none of his enemies had come out of the bushes.

"Hello, Uncle Wiggily!" politely mewed Tommie and Joie, and each little cat bent the tip of his tail as if making a bow.

"We saw you trying to get some apples," said Tommie, "and we came over to help you."

"That is very jolly and kind of you," said the rabbit uncle. "If you will help me gather some apples, Nurse Jane will give each of you a piece of the pie she is going to bake."

"Oh, how fine!" mewed Joie.

"I suppose you pussies would rather have milk, though, than pie," added Mr. Longears.

"Oh, we like pie, too, especially apple pie!" answered Tommie. "We'll help you pick the apples."

"I have not yet picked any," said Uncle Wiggily. "I can't reach them, and I can't knock or shake them down."

"We can climb the tree and pick them," mewed Joie.

The two pussy boys then stuck their sharp claws into the bark on the trunk of the tree and began to climb up into the branches, where the apples hung with their red cheeks shining in the sun.

"I am glad you two little cats came along, instead of Jackie and Peetie Bow Wow," Uncle Wiggily said as he watched Tommie and Joie climbing up. "Puppy dogs cannot climb trees."

"Yes, we are good tree-climbers," mewed Tommie, though he did not speak too proudly. He and his brother were now well up into the tree where the best apples grew.

"You sit down under the tree, Uncle Wiggily," purred Tommie, "and Joie and I will claw off the apples and drop them into your lap."

The rabbit sat on the green grass under the tree, waiting and waiting and waiting. All of a sudden an apple fell and hit him on the leg.

"Ugh!" grunted Uncle Wiggily.

"Oh, excuse me!" cried Joie. "That apple slipped out of my paw!"

"All right. I will excuse you!" said Mr. Longears, rubbing his leg. He sat on the grass under the tree a little longer. Then, all at once, down fell another apple, striking him on his back.

"Ouch!" cried the rabbit.

"I beg your pardon!" Tommie purred. "That apple slipped out of my paw!"

"Oh, I forgive you," answered Uncle Wiggily with a smile as he rubbed his back against the trunk of the tree. Then he picked up the two apples that had fallen, thinking how good Nurse Jane's pie would taste. All of a sudden, two more apples fell together, striking on the rabbit's head and bouncing off.

"Ouch! Ouch!" cried Mr. Longears, for they were very hard apples.

"Excuse us!" mewed Tommie and Joie. "That was a double slip!"

"Then I shall have to double my forgiveness!" and Uncle Wiggily laughed. "I think," he added, "that I shall not sit under this tree any more. It is too dangerous. I think we can gather apples some other way than by having you claw them off to drop on me."

"How else can we get the apples?" asked Joie.

"If I had a long rope," answered Uncle Wiggily, "I could throw it over the end of the lowest branch, where one of you could tie it fast. Then, if you and I pulled on the rope, we could shake the branch, and the apples would fall to the ground without hitting any of us."

"But where can we find a rope?" mewed Tommie.

"Over in the woods," answered Uncle Wiggily. "In the woods many wild grapevines grow. The vines are long and thin, like ropes, and they are strong. Come and help me get one of them."

Down out of the apple tree climbed Joie and Tommie. In the woods Uncle Wiggily used his sharp teeth to bite off a long piece of grapevine.

"I think this vine is long enough," said the rabbit, looking at the piece he had chewed off. "I do not need any more. Help me pull it to the apple tree."

The two pussies helped Uncle Wiggily pull the long grapevine to the apple tree. One end of the vine rope was fastened to the outer end of a branch on which hung many red-cheeked apples. Then, standing out of the way, Uncle Wiggily, Tommie, and Joie pulled on the vine rope, shaking the branch and making the apples fall to the ground in a red shower.

"We have apples enough, now, for many pies," said the bunny uncle with a happy laugh.

Then, all of a sudden, out of the woods rushed the black Bear. He was hungrily rubbing his black tongue on his white, sharp teeth.

"How dare you take my apples?" growled the Bear.

"Oh, are these your apples?" asked Uncle Wiggily. He was afraid of the Bear.

"Gurr! Gurr! Gurr! Yes! Yes! Of course these are my apples!" growled the Bear. "How dare you shake them down? I was saving them for applesauce! Now I am going to take all three of you off to my den! Gurr! Gurr! Gurr!"

"Oh, dear me!" mewed poor Tommie, too frightened to run.

"What shall we do?" mewed Joie, who was almost as afraid as a little mouse.

"You can't do anything!" growled the Bear, most impolitely, as he crashed his way through the bushes.

But Uncle Wiggily did do something.

Quick as a flash the rabbit gentleman began running around the Bear, who was now out of the bushes, standing in the long grass by the trunk of the apple tree. As he ran, Uncle Wiggily pulled after him the grapevine rope which was still tied to the branch of the tree. Still running in a circle, the bunny twisted the strong vine around and around the Bear and the tree, fastening the Bear tightly to the tree trunk.

"Stop! Stop! What are you doing?" howled the Bear.

"I am fixing you so that you cannot eat any of us!" answered the rabbit, bravely.

When Uncle Wiggily had finished running around, the Bear was so tightly bound to the tree that he could not run or get his paws loose.

"Quick now, boys! Gather up the pie apples and run!" called Uncle Wiggily. "Run fast!"

He and Joie and Tommie ran away from the Bear. It was five minutes before the Bear could untangle himself from the grape-vine rope.

"Gurr! Gurr! Gurr!" growled the hungry animal, as he went back to his den. "Uncle Wiggily is a very smart rabbit. But some day I shall catch him!" The Bear was always boasting like this.

Nurse Jane made a very fine pie from the apples the rabbit gentleman and the pussy boys had gathered. Tommie and Joie each had a large piece — not too large, you know, only just large enough.

"I think Uncle Wiggily should have two pieces!" squeaked Nurse Jane. She gave them to the rabbit gentleman, and he thanked her and ate them up.

But there was no pie for the Bear.

A Flag for Wood Land

Find out who was afraid of the fox.

BEFORE the leaves began to fall, Uncle Wiggily came back from the farm to his hollow stump bungalow. One day, soon after he came back, Jimmie Wibblewobble, the boy duck, was watching the rabbit gentleman bite a large piece of white bark from a birch tree.

"Are you going to make a canoe-boat of that bark as the Indians used to do?" quacked Jimmie.

"No, I am not going to make a canoe-boat," answered Mr. Longears, as he pulled the last edge of the bark free of the tree. "I am going to make a flag."

"What is a flag for?" asked the duck boy. It would seem that he had never turned his head to look up at flags which flutter from high poles.

"A flag is for many things," the rabbit answered. "Soldiers carry flags, when they fight, to make them remember their country. You might say that a flag means something fine to think about."

"I can think of grass-candy and corn-meal ice cream without a flag!" quacked Jimmie. "Those are fine things, aren't they?"

"No! No!" said Uncle Wiggily. "A flag does not stand for anything to eat. You will see what I mean when I have made our flag. Just wait!"

"Oh, so it is to be our flag. I am to have a part in it, am I?" asked Jimmie, pleased with the idea.

"Of course," answered Mr. Longears. "The flag I am going to make will be the flag of all of us who live here in Wood Land."

With sticky gum from the pine tree, Uncle Wiggily fastened to a pole the square of white birch bark he had bitten off the birch. With the red juice of a beet, which he dug in his garden, the rabbit gentleman made a picture of a rose on the flag. With the blue color from a forget-me-not flower, Uncle Wiggily drew the picture of a little house above the red rose on the white birch bark.

When he had finished this, the white birch bark flag, with its pictures of the rose and the house, was very pretty. Uncle Wiggily held the flag up for Jimmie to look at. When they had both admired it, Mr. Longears thrust the end of the flagpole into the soft earth.

"Hurrah!" cried Uncle Wiggily, standing on his tiptoes and taking off his hat. "Hurrah! Three cheers for our flag! When danger comes, we shall gather around our flag. Then we shall be brave and drive away the enemy!"

"Oh, does a flag make you brave?" quacked Jimmie, who was now paddling with his yellow, webbed feet in a mud-puddle.

"I hope our flag will make us all brave," said the rabbit. "It certainly should."

Then the other animal boys and girls gathered in the wood, near the rabbit's hollow stump bungalow to look at Uncle Wiggily's new flag. They all asked questions about it. Jimmie talked most about it, because he had seen the flag made.

"The flag is here for us to gather around. It will make us brave when danger comes," the boy duck quacked. "Ho! I feel brave already!" He moved his tail from side to side and stretched out his wings.

"I think I'm a little brave, too!" said Johnnie Bushytail, the squirrel.

"So am I!" barked Jackie Bow Wow, the puppy.

"There is no enemy here now, so what is the use of being brave?" mewed Kittie Kat, the pussy girl.

"Oh!" barked Jackie. "Girls don't know anything about soldiers and flags and being brave, do they, Jimmie?"

"No, I guess they don't!" quacked Jimmie.

The flag fluttered in the wind. No enemies came near it. Uncle Wiggily and his friends were safe.

But one day there was real danger in Wood Land. The danger came from a big, hungry Fox who lived in a den in the forest. The fox wanted to catch Uncle Wiggily and eat him. Sniffing and snuffing down a path through the woods along which the rabbit had hopped, the Fox at last came near to the hollow stump bungalow.

"That is where Uncle Wiggily lives!" growled the Fox. "A duck lives near him, too. I can see the marks of the duck's paddle-feet in the soft mud. I shall catch Uncle Wiggily and perhaps a duck, too! Oh, I am so hungry!"

The Fox hid beneath a spice bush and looked down at the rabbit's bungalow.

"I will wait a little while for him to come out," said the hungry Fox. "If he does not come out soon, I will smash his bungalow and get him that way. I wonder what that is fluttering there in front of the bungalow."

The Fox looked at the flag, but he did not know what it was. "No matter," he growled. "It can't be anything to harm me." So the Fox hid under the spice bush.

The Ruffed Grouse, a fine, big bird, flew through the air over the spice bush and saw the Fox hiding there.

"I must tell Uncle Wiggily that an enemy is after him!" thought the Ruffed Grouse. He flew over the bungalow, beating his wings, like tiny drums to warn the rabbit, but Mr. Longears was asleep.

Then the Ruffed Grouse told the Robin about the Fox under the spice bush.

"Try to warn Uncle Wiggily!" begged the Grouse.

Around the bungalow flew the Robin, singing:

"Get up! Get up! Get up, Uncle Wiggily!"

Still the rabbit slept, nor did he awaken when other birds called to him, for they all saw the Fox.

"What can we do?" asked the Ruffed Grouse.

The Fox was now getting more and more hungry, so he began to creep closer to the rabbit's bungalow. Then Sammie Little-tail, the rabbit boy, came hopping by on his way home from school. He saw the Fox.

"I must run fast and tell Uncle Wiggily!" thought Sammie.

Through the forest, away from the spice bush which was upon a hill over the bungalow, ran Sammie. He saw Uncle Wiggily, who had just awakened, come slowly out on his front porch to look at the red, white, and blue flag fluttering in the wind.

"Danger! Danger!" cried Sammie. "The Fox is creeping out from under the spice bush! He is coming to get you, Uncle Wiggily! Danger! Danger!"

"Ho! Ho!" loudly called the rabbit gentleman. "If there is danger, we must all gather around the flag and drive the enemy away! Ho, my friends! Come to where the flag flies in the wind and drive away the Fox!"

All who heard Uncle Wiggily's voice left their homes, their work, or their play. Together they gathered at the side of the bungalow where the birch bark flag fluttered in the wind.

Nearer and nearer crept the hungry Fox. He had a red tongue that curled over his white teeth. His teeth were sharp, and he was hungry.

"I shall soon be eating a fat rabbit or a juicy duck!" thought the Fox. "Then I shall no longer feel hungry."

Uncle Wiggily looked at his friends who were gathered near the flag. Sammie and Susie Littletail, the rabbit children, were there. Johnnie and Billie Bushytail, the squirrels, curled their big tails over their backs. Nannie and Billie Wagtail, the goats, were also there. So were Josie, Tommie, and Kittie Kat.

"I have brought my bag of marbles," mewed Tommie. "I will throw hard marbles at the Fox and drive him away."

"I will throw my spinning top at the Fox," said Billie the squirrel. "If the sharp peg of my top hits the Fox on the nose, he will run."

"Maybe he will run if I make my doll squeak at him," said Susie, the rabbit girl, and no one laughed at her.

Uncle Wiggily counted his friends who were gathered around the flag.

"There are not enough of us," said the rabbit, whose pink nose was not twinkling very much now, for he was frightened. "We must have more to drive away the Fox. Ho! Ho! Come and help!" cried the rabbit gentleman.

"Ha! Ha!" said the Fox. "He can never get enough help to drive me away. I have never before seen so many good things to eat. Let me see, which one shall I take first?" He sat down in the shade of a big rock to think.

Again and again Uncle Wiggily called for more of his friends to gather around the flag and drive away the Fox. At last the rabbit's voice grew tired, and he could call no longer.

"We need more help," said Uncle Wiggily, as he saw the Fox again creeping slowly toward him. The Fox had made up his mind to eat the rabbit first and, after that, everyone else.

"We need more help, but who will call for it?" asked the rabbit.

Suddenly the Ruffed Grouse, who had flown to seek more birds to help, came fluttering back. He heard Uncle Wiggily ask for someone else to call for help.

"I will!" cried the Grouse. "I will beat my drum, and all who hear it echoing in the woods will come to drive away the Fox!"

The bird beat his wings on his breast, making a sound like two drums.

"Boom! Boom! Boom!" called the Ruffed Grouse.

Hearing this, many more friends of Uncle Wiggily hurried through the forest to drive away the Fox. They gathered around the flag.

"Where is Jackie Bow Wow? Where is Peetie Bow Wow?" called the rabbit gentleman. "Why are those two little puppy dog boys not here to help us drive away the Fox?"

Then up spoke Susie Littletail, the rabbit girl.

"I saw Jackie and Peetie!" she cried. "They said they were
afraid of the Fox and were going to hide in their kennel house."

"Oh, that must never be!" said Uncle Wiggily. "Jackie and
Peetie must not be afraid! They must be brave and stand by our
flag!"

Looking toward the kennel house, Mr. Longears called:

"Come out, Jackie and Peetie! Come out! Be brave! Help
us drive away the Fox!"

Then Jackie and Peetie felt sorry for what they had done.
They ran out of their kennel house. They had hidden their tails
between their legs, but at the sound of Uncle Wiggily's brave
voice, and at the sight of the fluttering flag, the puppy dogs
raised their tails high in the air.

"We will fight the Fox!" they barked.

The Fox rushed out from behind the rock. He tried to get
Uncle Wiggily. Jackie bit him on one leg. Peetie bit him on
another leg. Tommie Kat threw hard marbles at the Fox. With
his spinning top, Billie Bushytail hit the Fox on the nose. Susie
Littletail made her doll squeak loudly at the Fox, and that helped.

But it was the bites of Jackie and Peetie that turned the Fox back and made him afraid.

"Oh! Ouch! Oh, dear!" howled the Fox, and, with the two little puppy dog boys snapping at his heels, he ran back to his den in the forest.

"Now we are saved!" said Uncle Wiggily. "You were very brave, Jackie and Peetie!"

"We felt brave when we saw you standing by our flag," barked the doggie boys. "It showed us how strong we can be when we all stand and work together."

"Three cheers for our flag!" called Uncle Wiggily.

I wish you could have heard those animal girls and boys cheer! The Fox heard it, and it made him run the faster.

"There must be something magical about a flag," growled the Fox to himself, as he hid in a dark corner of his den. "I wonder what it can be?"

Uncle Wiggily's Snow Sled

Find out how Uncle Wiggily made a sled.

ALL OVER the Wood Land the ground was covered with snow. All around the rabbit's hollow stump bungalow the earth was white.

"I must be careful when I hop out to look for an adventure today," said Uncle Wiggily to himself as he drew on his rubber boots. "My feet will leave very plain marks in the snow. The Fox, the Wolf, the Bob Cat, and the Bear can easily see my footprints and track me through the snow. I must be careful!"

As he hopped along, Uncle Wiggily looked first on this side of the path and then on that side, to make sure no enemies were hiding behind the snowy bushes to leap out at him.

After hopping about a mile through the snow, Uncle Wiggily reached a long hill. Around it he heard the sounds of shouts and laughter.

"Those jolly noises are not made by any of my enemies," thought the rabbit uncle. "The boy and girl animals are having fun sliding downhill. Let me stop to watch them."

Hopping through the edge of the woods, Mr. Longears soon reached the top of the coasting hill. There were many animal children sliding down on their sleds, making the air ring with their merry laughter. As soon as they saw Uncle Wiggily, they called out to him.

"Come and ride with us! Come and coast downhill!" they shouted.

"Oh, I am too old for that!" answered the rabbit gentleman.

"No! No! You are not too old! You will never get too old!" barked Jackie Bow Wow.

"You grow younger every day you live!" bleated Uncle Butter. The goat gentleman had also stopped at the coasting hill to see the fun. "I think looking for adventures keeps you young, Uncle Wiggily."

"Perhaps it does," said the rabbit, nodding his head.

Again the children called:

"Come and coast with us!"

"Ride on my sled!" shouted Johnnie Bushytail.

"Take mine!" mewed Tommie Kat.

"Well, I thought I was too old ever to coast again!" said Mr. Longears. "If Uncle Butter will ride with me, I'll go down just once."

"I'll ride!" said the goat.

"Hurrah! Hurrah!" shouted the boys and girls. "Uncle Wiggily and Uncle Butter are going to ride down the hill!"

Both the rabbit and the goat sat on Jackie Bow Wow's sled. Tommie Kat and his brother Joie gave a push. Down the long, snowy hill rushed Uncle Wiggily and the goat.

"This is great fun!" cried Mr. Longears.

"Lots of fun!" bleated Uncle Butter.

When they reached the bottom, they jumped off the sled and pulled it up the hill. They liked the ride so much that they went down again, and even a third time.

Then Uncle Butter said he must go to the store to get some potatoes for Aunt Lettie. Mr. Longears remembered that Nurse Jane had asked him to stop at the coop of Mrs. Cluck-Cluck and get a dozen eggs. So the two friends thanked the animal boys for their ride and left the hill together.

Uncle Wiggily took the eggs to his bungalow. Later that afternoon, when the muskrat housekeeper was baking a cake, she heard a bumping noise in the cellar.

"Hello!" she squeaked. "Who is down there?"

"I am!" answered Uncle Wiggily. "It's all right. I am just looking for something."

"I wonder what he is looking for?" thought Miss Fuzzy Wuzzy, as she beat up the eggs for the cake. She looked out of the back window and saw Uncle Wiggily hopping away with a wooden washtub over his head.

"What in the world is that funny rabbit going to do now?" Nurse Jane asked herself with a laugh. "I suppose he is going to make some sort of a playhouse for the children. He will never grow up!"

Uncle Wiggily was not going to make a playhouse out of the tub. He was going to make a sled, but he did not want Nurse Jane to know it.

"If I were not so old," said Uncle Wiggily to himself, when he had come back from coasting on the hill with Uncle Butter, "if I were not so old, I would buy myself a sled. I like to coast on the snow. But I am too old!"

Suddenly, he thought of the wooden washtubs in his cellar.

"Ha!" he cried softly. "If I could fasten some runners on a tub, it would be like a sled. Then I could ride downhill as much as I pleased without anyone's laughing at me. There is a little hill back of my bungalow. I could coast there all by myself and no one would see me. Ha! I'll do it!"

He took the tub out of the cellar and fastened on some strips of wood for runners.

"Now I'll see how it rides!" said the rabbit.

He sat on his funny sled at the top of the hill, gave himself a push, and down he went just as nicely as you please.

"Ho! Ho! This is fun!" laughed Mr. Longears. "I must show Uncle Butter how to make a sled like this. After all, I am not too old to have a good time coasting."

When he reached the bottom, he climbed to the top again, hauling his tub-sled up by a piece of wild grapevine. Again and again Mr. Longears coasted down until it was getting dark. Then he thought he had ridden enough for that day.

"I'll take one last ride and then go home," he thought.

Now from the top of another hill the Fox, the Wolf, and the Bob Cat had seen Uncle Wiggily coasting in his funny sled.

"That old rabbit is turning young again!" growled the Wolf.

"He thinks he is a boy!" said the Bob Cat.

"Listen!" whispered the sly Fox. "When Uncle Wiggily is in that tub, his legs are curled up, and he can't get out quickly to run. This is our chance to catch him!"

"Yes! Yes! We shall catch him!" howled the Wolf and the Bob Cat.

The three hungry animals ran to the bottom of the hill just as Uncle Wiggily started down from the top on his last ride. Too late the bunny saw his three enemies waiting for him. So eager and hungry were they that they did not stay at the bottom of the hill. They ran up the slippery place.

Down rushed the washtub-sled with the rabbit in it.

"Clear the track! Get out of my way!" cried Uncle Wiggily.

"We are going to catch you this time!" howled the three hungry ones.

But the tub was going so fast, and the hill was so slippery, that, all of a sudden, the funny sled slid against the Fox, the Wolf, and the Bob Cat, knocking them down, bumping them along, and turning them heads over paws down the hill. Safely past them coasted Uncle Wiggily.

"Oh, oh! He bumped my nose!" howled the Bob Cat.

"Oh, oh! He bumped my head!" growled the Wolf.

"Oh, oh! He bumped my back!" cried the Fox.

The three animals were knocked off to one side of the hill and into the deep snow. Uncle Wiggily coasted safely to the bottom of the hill. Then, before the Fox, the Wolf, and the Bob Cat could get out of the snow and run after him, the rabbit hopped to his bungalow and locked the door.

"Now I am all right," said the rabbit gentleman when he told Nurse Jane what had happened. "I rode downhill in my tub-sled. I had a fine adventure and now I am safe at home. What more could I want?"

Billie's Beans

Find out how Billie's beans were spilled.

ONE SPRING morning Nurse Jane Fuzzy Wuzzy gave Uncle Wiggily carrot pancakes for breakfast. The rabbit gentleman was eating them slowly and politely, thinking of the adventures he might have that day.

"Look here!" squeaked Nurse Jane.

"Look where?" Uncle Wiggily wanted to know. He glanced toward one of the bungalow windows.

"I don't see anything!" he told the muskrat lady housekeeper.

"What did you think you would see?" asked Nurse Jane.

"I thought you wanted me to look at the Fox or Wolf trying to climb in to bite me," said Mr. Longears.

"Oh, no!" and Nurse Jane laughed at the idea. "I just meant for you to look at this." She was holding up a little bag of red silk. "Isn't it pretty?"

"Yes, but what is it?"

"This is Sister Sallie's sewing bag," answered Miss Fuzzy Wuzzy. "Sister Sallie is the little rabbit girl who sometimes comes over here to play with Susie Littletail and Baby Bunty. The animal girls were playing house in your bungalow yesterday, and Sister Sallie forgot her sewing bag."

"Well, I am going to look for an adventure, as I do nearly every day," said Uncle Wiggily. "If you want me to, I will take Sister Sallie's sewing bag to her. She may want to sew a new dress for her doll."

Nurse Jane swung the red silk bag on the end of her paw.

"Yes," the muskrat lady said, "there are needles, thread, a thimble, and some pieces of cloth in Sister Sallie's sewing bag. She could easily make a doll's dress from what is here and have some cloth and thread left over."

Nurse Jane folded up the red bag carefully, tied the strings around it, and handed it to the rabbit gentleman. Then Uncle Wiggily, with his red, white, and blue crutch, began hopping along the path through the woods, taking the sewing bag to the little rabbit girl.

As he reached a shady place, where the green grass grew very thick and there was green moss on the rocks and trees, he saw the Robin sitting on the branch of a white birch tree. The Robin sang this song:

I sit up high in the apple tree!
  Cheer-up! Cheer-up! Cheer-up!
I swing so gaily, light and free!
  Cheer-up! Cheer-up! Cheer-up!
The sun shines bright on the apples red.
I'll drop one on the Blackbird's head.
For Summer has come since Winter has fled—
  Cheer-up! Cheer-up! Cheer-up!

"That was a nice song Mr. Robin!" called out Uncle Wiggily, for he knew it was the Daddy Robin who was doing the singing. Mother Robin is too busy making a nest, laying eggs, and hatching out little birds, to do much singing.

"I am glad you liked my song!" whistled Mr. Robin, holding his head up higher.

"But, about dropping an apple on the Blackbird's head," went on Mr. Longears, anxiously. "Are you sure it will not hurt the Blackbird?"

"Tra-la-la!" sang Mr. Robin. "That was only a joke! I am not really going to drop an apple on my friend Mr. Blackbird. He has red spots on his wings, brighter than the red feathers on my breast, so he is called Redwing Blackbird. It was only a little joke about hitting him on the head with an apple. I wouldn't do it for the world!"

"You are quite merry this morning!" said Uncle Wiggily.

"Yes — and no!" sang the bird. "I am glad because the sun shines and because it is summer. But I am worried about the nest Mrs. Robin and I are making in the old apple tree. We cannot find enough bits of string, rags, and other things to finish our nest. My wife is flying around now, looking for pieces of soft cloth or thread. As soon as I finish another song, I shall help her. It is my duty to sing first, to cheer her a bit."

"Perhaps I can help you with something from this bag," spoke Uncle Wiggily, holding up the red silk bag he was taking back to Sister Sallie. "In this bag are many more bits of thread and cloth than the little rabbit girl will need for a doll's dress. I will give you some if you like."

"Oh, thank you!" whistled the Robin, ending his song with a beautiful little trill. "Thank you very much!"

On the end of his red, white, and blue crutch the rabbit gentleman laid some pieces of soft silk and bits of thread from the spools in the bag. Then he raised the crutch up toward the limb of the tree where the Robin was perched. The bird quickly picked off the cloth and threads in his beak.

"These will finish our nest nicely," he said to the rabbit, and he flew away to tell Mrs. Robin the good news. Long threads trailed through the air from the Robin's beak as he flew.

Uncle Wiggily watched the bird for a few minutes. Then, twinkling his pink nose, he hopped along until he reached the hollow log house where Sister Sallie lived. Sallie was at school, but the mother rabbit said she was sure her little girl would be glad that Mr. Longears had given some of the sewing things to the Robin.

"Now I must look for my daily adventure," said Mr. Longears to himself, as he called "Good-by!" to Sallie's mother. "It is getting late."

In the soft, dark, shadowy woods the rabbit stopped to look at a wild grapevine, thinking what a fine swing it would make for the animal boys and girls. All at once he heard a noise in the bushes.

"I hope that isn't the Fox or the Bob Cat!" thought the rabbit uncle. He had to be on guard against enemies, you see.

Just then, out of the bushes jumped Billie Bushytail, the boy squirrel, carrying a paper bag.

"Hello, Uncle Wiggily!" chattered Billie.

"Hello!" answered the bunny rabbit gentleman. "What have you there?"

"There are beans in this bag," answered the squirrel. "I just bought them at the store for my mother. See how strong I am!" As he said this, Billie raised the bag of beans high over his head.

"Be careful! You'll drop those beans!" cried Uncle Wiggily.

The warning came too late. Billie's paw slipped. The bag fell to the ground. It struck on a sharp stone and burst open. All the beans spilled out.

"Oh! Oh!!" cried poor Billie.

"Dear me!" sighed Uncle Wiggily.

"What am I going to do?" asked the squirrel boy.

"You must pick up the beans," answered Mr. Longears. "I will help you. I will make you another bag by fastening together some of the large leaves from the wild grapevine. I can fasten the leaves together with sticky gum from the pine tree."

"Thank you!" said Billie in a low voice. He did not feel very strong now. He wished he had not lifted the bag so high, and he was sorry he had boasted. But it was too late.

Uncle Wiggily and Billie began picking up the beans. There were a great many of them scattered all about on the ground. Only one bean could be picked up at a time, for dirt and stones would be gathered up by the paws of the rabbit gentleman and the squirrel boy if they tried to pick up a number of beans at once.

"We can put the beans in my hat until we have them all picked up," said Uncle Wiggily. "Then I will make the leaf bag to hold them."

"It is very slow work, picking up one bean at a time," said Billie.

It seemed that all the beans would never be gathered. Billie's back began to ache. Mr. Longears also was tired. He wished Billie had not tried to show how strong he was.

Suddenly there sounded a fluttering in the leaves of the tree near where many of the beans had spilled, and down flew three birds.

"Who are you?" asked Uncle Wiggily, dropping a bean as he spoke.

"Why, don't you remember me?" whistled the Robin, who was one of the three birds. "I was singing a song for you a little while ago. You most kindly gave me some thread and bits of cloth to help me and my wife to build our nest. This is Mrs. Robin," and he fluttered a wing at the other red-breasted bird.

"And this is my friend, Mr. Redwing Blackbird," added the Robin, nodding his head at the third singer. "I did not drop any apples on his head," added Mr. Robin, slyly.

"I am glad of that!" said Mr. Longears, hardly knowing what was going to happen.

"We have come to help you and Billie pick up the beans," Mrs. Robin chirped. "We were flying high in the air, Mr. Robin and I, and we saw what happened. So we called for Mr. Blackbird and flew down to help you. You helped us to build a nest, Uncle Wiggily, so now we want to help you and Billie gather the spilled beans."

"This is very kind of you!" said Mr. Longears. "Billie and I were getting very tired."

With their sharp beaks, the three birds could pick up the beans much more quickly than could the rabbit and squirrel. The birds picked up one bean at a time and did not gather up any dirt or stones. Soon all the beans except two large red ones were put into Uncle Wiggily's hat.

"You may have one red bean, Mr. Blackbird," said the bunny rabbit. "It matches the red spots on your wings. You may have the other red bean, Mr. and Mrs. Robin."

"Oh, thank you!" chirped Mrs. Robin. "I will save it to hang on a necklace which I shall weave of sweet grass when I hatch out a little girl robin."

"I hope I may see it," said Uncle Wiggily politely.

Then Mr. Longears made a green leaf bag for Billie to carry the beans in to his mother.

As the birds flew away the Robin whistled:

Sing high! Sing low!
Let the whole world know
When Robin sings his song.
He sings at morn; he sings at noon;
He sings at night a bedtime tune.
He marks the day
Singing his lay—
But he never sings too long!

Mending a Roof

Find out why Nurse Jane went with Uncle Wiggily to mend the roof.

T HE RED-BREASTED Robin flew down out of a tree. Merrily he whistled a song as he left a letter at the nest-house of Mr. Caw Caw, the black crow gentleman.

"Tra-la-la! Tra-la-la!" sang the Robin, and then he whistled:

There's none in the world
Quite so happy as I,
For I sing on my way
As I mount to the sky!

"Where are you going next, Mr. Robin?" called the black crow.

"To Uncle Wiggily's hollow stump bungalow," answered the Robin. "I have a letter for the rabbit gentleman."

Mr. Robin was the letter carrier of Wood Land. On he flew, fluttering his wings in the sunshine.

"Thank you," said Uncle Wiggily when the Robin gave him a letter.

"It is a pleasure to bring it to you!" chirped Mr. Robin as he flew on to leave a note for Aunt Lettie the goat.

93

"From whom is your letter, Uncle Wiggily?" asked Nurse Jane.
The note was written on very thin white bark from the birch
tree, and was inside a piece of stronger bark, folded in the shape
of an envelope. On the envelope was written, in ink made from
the juice of a blackberry, the name:

MR. WIGGILY LONGEARS

"The letter is from my friend, Uncle Butter, the goat," answered Mr. Longears, when he had opened the bark envelope and
taken out the note. "I shall read it to you, Miss Fuzzy Wuzzy."
This is what the letter said:

Wood Land, May 1

Dear Uncle Wiggily,
Will you please come over tomorrow and help me mend the roof
of my house? There is a big hole in the roof and the rain drips through
it. Sometimes the drops splash on my nose. Please come as soon as
you can.

Your friend,
Uncle Butter

"Are you going?" asked Nurse Jane.

"Of course I am going!" answered Mr. Longears. "Uncle Butter is my friend and neighbor. Friends and neighbors must help one another. I shall hop over to Uncle Butter's house tomorrow and help him mend his roof."

It was then late in the afternoon, too late to go look for an adventure. So, after he had dug some carrots out of his garden for supper, Uncle Wiggily went to bed.

"Tomorrow I shall get up early," he thought, "and help my goat friend mend his roof."

Before Uncle Wiggily fell asleep, all of a sudden he heard the rain pattering on the roof of his hollow stump bungalow.

"I am glad my roof is snug and tight!" thought the rabbit gentleman to himself. "No rain can get in to wet me!"

Then he remembered Uncle Butter.

"Oh, but the rain will come in the goat's house!" cried Mr. Longears, jumping out of bed. "There is a hole in Uncle Butter's roof! I must hop over at once and help him mend it. I shall not wait for tomorrow!"

"You can't go out in all this rain!" squeaked Nurse Jane as she heard Uncle Wiggily hopping around in his room, getting dressed. "It is raining very hard!"

"I must go out!" said the bunny uncle. "Think of poor Uncle Butter and Mrs. Wagtail and Aunt Lettie and Billie and Nannie with the rain dripping in on them! I must go and help mend the roof before they are all wet through and through!"

"Well, I suppose it will be a kind thing to do," squeaked Nurse Jane.

Uncle Wiggily put on his coat, looked for his umbrella, and started out in the dark and storm. He carried with him his bottle of fireflies for a lantern.

Now some of the other animals in Wood Land were not as kind as Uncle Wiggily. Some were cruel because it was their nature to be that way. They could not help it. Among these cruel animals were the Wolf and the Fox.

As the rain pattered down on the leaves of the trees, the Wolf crept from his den to that of the Fox next door.

"Come out, Mr. Fox!" growled the Wolf.

"Why should I come out in all this rain?" asked the Fox.

"Because it will be the best time to catch Uncle Wiggily," the Wolf answered. "We can go to his hollow stump bungalow now. The rain will make such a noise on his roof that he will not hear us when we smash one of the windows to crawl in. Come with me. A rainy night is the best time to catch that rabbit!"

"All right," grumbled the Fox, "but it is a bad night to be out."

The Wolf and the Fox started for Uncle Wiggily's bungalow, but before they reached it, the rabbit gentleman had hopped out to go and help Uncle Butter mend the hole in his roof.

Nurse Jane went with Uncle Wiggily. When the muskrat lady saw Mr. Longears hopping out into the dark, rainy night, she squeaked:

"I am not going to stay here all alone, without even Baby Bunty to keep me company. I am coming with you, Uncle Wiggily. Perhaps I can help you mend the hole in Uncle Butter's roof."

"Perhaps you can," said the rabbit gentleman. "Come along."

So Nurse Jane put on her raincoat and went with him.

Besides carrying his umbrella, Uncle Wiggily had some flat pieces of birch bark, such as the Indians used to make their canoe-boats, and the rabbit also had some sticky gum from the pine tree.

"With the bark and the gum I can put a patch over the hole in Uncle Butter's roof," said the bunny rabbit gentleman as he and Nurse Jane splashed their way along the path through the woods. The firefly lantern did not give very much light, and often Mr. Longears and Nurse Jane stepped into mud-puddles. But they did not mind.

It was not very far to the goat gentleman's house. Mr. Long-ears and the muskrat lady were soon there.

"Hello, Uncle Butter!" called Uncle Wiggily in a loud voice. He closed his umbrella, set the firefly lantern down on the steps, and knocked on the door. "Hello! Hello!"

"Hello, down there!" bleated the goat, putting his head out of an upstairs window. "Who is down there in all the rain?"

"I am!" answered Uncle Wiggily. "Nurse Jane and I are here to help you mend the hole in your roof. Is the rain coming in very fast?"

"Indeed it is!" bleated Aunt Lettie. "I am catching as much as I can in the dishpan and a washtub. You are a good neighbor, Uncle Wiggily, to come over in all this storm to help."

"I am glad to come," said Mr. Longears, wiping a raindrop out of his left eye. "That is what neighbors are for—to help others. If you will open the door, Uncle Butter, Nurse Jane and I will come in and see what we can do."

"Oh, excuse me!" bleated the goat gentleman. "I was so surprised at hearing you call that I forgot to let you in. Just wait a moment!"

He pulled in his head and horns, clattered downstairs, and opened the front door.

"Dear me! You are all wet!" cried Aunt Lettie, as she and Mrs. Wagtail hurried to find more pans and tubs to catch the water that was raining in through the hole in the roof.

"Oh, we don't mind that!" said Uncle Wiggily. "Now, Nurse Jane, you help Aunt Lettie and Mrs. Wagtail set pans to catch the rain, while Uncle Butter and I climb out on the roof to put the sticky birch bark over the hole."

The roof of the goat's house was not very high, and Uncle Wiggily and Mr. Butter got up on it from a ladder. Uncle Butter held the firefly lantern and Uncle Wiggily mended the hole.

"There! No more rain will come in!" cried Uncle Wiggily, as he slid gently down off the roof. Uncle Butter followed. When they went in the house, Aunt Lettie had some hot clover tea waiting for them.

While this was happening at the goat's house, the Fox and the Wolf had reached the hollow stump bungalow, walking softly through the rain in the dark woods.

"The rain is making such a noise that Uncle Wiggily will not hear us break one of his windows," said the Wolf, shaking the water from his tail.

"No," said the Fox. "We shall surely catch him this time!"

Suddenly there was a flash of lightning, and the thunder crashed. When the lightning had gone, leaving the woods darker than before, the Fox threw a stone through one of the bungalow windows. They quickly climbed in.

"Where are you, Uncle Wiggily?" growled the Wolf. "We have come to get you!"

"And Nurse Jane, too!" howled the Fox.

They ran through all the rooms with their muddy paws, but the Fox and the Wolf could find neither the rabbit gentleman nor the muskrat lady. Because, you know, they were safe at Uncle Butter's house, mending the roof.

"They've gone!" snapped the Wolf, rubbing his tongue over his sharp teeth, for he was very hungry.

"They played a trick on us!" howled the Fox. "We came out in all this rain for nothing! Gurr! Gurr! Gurr!"

Growling and snapping, the two angry and hungry animals went back to their dens, getting wetter than ever.

After the storm was over, next morning, Uncle Wiggily and Nurse Jane went back to their hollow stump bungalow. When he saw the marks of the muddy paws in all the rooms, Uncle Wiggily said:

"It was a good thing we went to mend Uncle Butter's roof last night. See, the Fox and the Wolf called on us!"

"Well," squeaked Nurse Jane with a laugh, "I'm glad we were not at home!"

Uncle Wiggily's Enemies

Find out where Uncle Wiggily's enemies went.

ONE DAY Uncle Wiggily lay down in the warm spring sun-shine near his hollow stump bungalow and fell fast asleep. He slept so soundly that he did not hear a rustling in the grass and leaves which might have told him that some hungry animals were coming to eat him. The animals were gathering around the sleeping rabbit.

First came the sly Weasel, who rubbed his white teeth with his red tongue and whispered:

"I wonder which of his ears I shall bite first."

Then up crept the Wolf. He sat down a little way from Uncle Wiggily, looked hungrily at the rabbit, and growled in a low voice.

"I come before you, Mr. Weasel, for I am bigger and stronger than you ever will be!"

"Yes, I suppose so," said the sly little beast. "But here comes someone else!" The Wolf and Weasel turned to see the Fox running toward them.

"Am I too late?" asked the Fox. "I heard the Bob Cat say Uncle Wiggily was here asleep, and I came to get my share of him."

"We haven't begun yet," growled the Wolf. "You are in plenty of time."

"Wait for me! Wait for me! Don't begin to eat until I get there!" suddenly cried a voice, and up rushed the Bob Cat with his silly little tail.

"I want some too!" called a deep voice, and along shuffled the Bear. "I am the largest of all," he said, "so I shall take the first bite."

"There will be little left for us when the Bear is finished," whispered the Weasel.

102

"Stand back now!" roared the Bear, walking closer to the sleeping rabbit, and shaking his paws at the other animals. "Don't any of you dare to take a nibble until I have had my share!"

The loud voice of the Bear awakened Uncle Wiggily. He rubbed his sleepy eyes with his paws, and sat up.

Then the rabbit saw all the hungry animals gathered around him. He gave one big, long jump and started running so fast that none of them could catch him.

As he ran, Uncle Wiggily kicked up a cloud of dust which hid him from sight until he had safely reached his hollow stump bungalow. In he hopped, locking the door.

"Well, I guess this is the end," said the Wolf. The hungry animals turned back from the clearing in the woods where the rabbit lived with his friends. "We shall never catch Uncle Wiggily."

"It was all the Bear's fault for growling so loud and waking him," whispered the Weasel.

"Indeed it was!" said the Bob Cat, sitting on his tail so that none of the others could see how small it was. "All the Bear's fault. And I, for one, don't like it."

"What's that? Who dares find fault with me?" growled the Bear, who was tired and angry from his useless run after Uncle Wiggily. "How dare you find fault with me?" growled the big animal.

With that he rushed at the Bob Cat, who ran away as fast as he could. Then the Bear darted after the Fox, but that wise animal found a hole into which he crawled, and the Wolf and the Weasel, seeing how angry the Bear was, also hid themselves.

"There is no use staying around here any more!" said the Bear, after a while, when Uncle Wiggily did not come out of

his bungalow. "I don't believe we can ever catch that rabbit. He is too smart for us. I am going off to a far country where rabbits are not so clever."

"We'll come, too!" said the Wolf, the Fox, the Weasel, and the Bob Cat, coming back to the path along which the Bear was shuffling away from the bunny's bungalow. "There is no use staying around here."

"Come along then!" growled the Bear. "We'll go to another part of the woods where we may have better luck!"

And the hungry animals marched over the hill and far away.

The next morning Uncle Butter, the goat gentleman, who had watched the Bear and his friends leaving Wood Land, told Uncle Wiggily about it.

"I do not believe," bleated the goat, "that you will have any more trouble, Mr. Longears."

"Well, I surely am glad of that!" said Uncle Wiggily. "Still, I had a pretty good time out of it all. I had adventures, and they kept me from getting old too fast. But I shall be glad of a rest— yes, indeed, I shall be glad of a rest."

Then the rabbit gentleman twinkled his pink nose and hopped slowly along under the green trees.

branches of the tree were suet and ears of yellow corn. There were pieces of bread, holders filled with sunflower seeds, nut meats and raisins. On the ground were chickfeed and cracked corn and bread crumbs.

"Dee, dee, dee!" cried Timmy Tit the Chicadee merrily.

"What cheer! What cheer!" called Glory the Cardinal, bursting into song as beautiful as his red coat.

Sammy Jay was there. So were Downy the Woodpecker and his cousin Hairy, and Yank Tank the Nuthatch. And Linnet the Purple Finch, Chicadee the Goldfinch, and Dotty the Tree Sparrow were all there, too.

All through the day there was happiness, and the little good will tree, no longer lonesome, was the happiest of all.

May good will prevail throughout the world this Christmas Day.

The Little Good Will Tree

THE young fir tree sighed softly, for it was lonesome. Over in the Green Forest were many young fir trees growing together and so keeping each other company. But here in Farmer Brown's dooryard the young fir was alone. Because no other trees were near to crowd it, the young tree had grown to be very beautiful. Farmer Brown's boy called it his all-year Christmas tree.

One afternoon, just before dark, Farmer Brown's boy visited the tree. The young fir tree was even more lonesome than usual because the big snow storm had kept his animal friends away. But then Farmer Brown's boy came out and started tying things to the little tree's branches. He was busy for some time, and then he left.

Suddenly the tree was lonesome no longer. First there came a great change in the weather and with it came all the little animal friends of the tree. Timmy the Flying Squirrel came, and little Whitefoot the Wood Mouse with dainty little white hands and feet was there. Blacky the Crow came just as jolly round, bright Mr. Sun began to climb up in the blue, blue sky to smile down on the young tree. And a million tiny frost crystals flashed and sparkled like jewels of happiness.

All day long feathered friends from the Old Orchard and the Green Forest kept coming and going. The little tree was lonesome no longer.

The little friends came to the tree hungry and anxious because of the storm. But they went away filled with food and happiness. For tied to the

BABY BEARS

MOTHER BEAR has her babies in the middle of winter. The babies are born in a cave, or under a pile of fallen trees, or perhaps under a snow-covered heap of brush. When the cubs are about three months old, they venture out to see what the world is like. Then they are the most mischievous, fun-loving scamps in all the Green Forest, and Mother Bear has her paws full. She sometimes spanks them and sends them up a tree when they have been naughty. But it is Mother Bear who teaches the little Bears what every Bear should know.

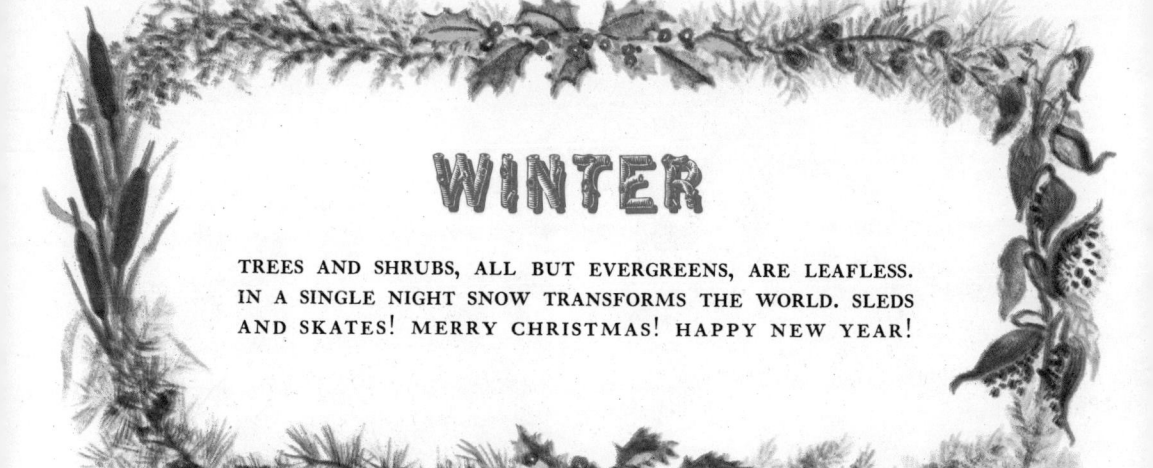

WINTER

TREES AND SHRUBS, ALL BUT EVERGREENS, ARE LEAFLESS. IN A SINGLE NIGHT SNOW TRANSFORMS THE WORLD. SLEDS AND SKATES! MERRY CHRISTMAS! HAPPY NEW YEAR!

Bobby Coon's Home

HERE is Bobby Coon in his little home in the hollow of a tree. Here Bobby Coon can live safe and sound, looking out upon the world.

But sometimes the wood choppers come and the tree is cut down. Bobby Coon loses his little home. Then Bobby Coon and his family must find another home in another tree. Fortunately, there are always plenty of trees.

Lightfoot's "Yard"

LIGHTFOOT the Deer is making what is called a yard. He has chosen a place where food is plentiful and there he has made a great number of paths crossing and recrossing in every direction. After each snowstorm he tramps these paths out. Then he will be able to get about no matter how deep the snow becomes during the winter. But he will have to stay in this "yard" when the snow becomes very deep.

time his small brother was leaning over and he, too, saw another little Coon.

"Who are you?" asked Spiketail. "And who are you?" asked his brother. But the two strangers in the water did not answer. Spiketail put out a paw. His little stranger friend put out a paw. The two paws seemed to meet, and yet they didn't, for Spiketail felt nothing but water. He drew back puzzled. The stranger drew back, too. And all the time, Little Bob was doing the same things on his side of the log with his stranger friend.

Suddenly Spiketail remembered what his mother had once told him about mirrors. "Why, we are just looking at ourselves in the pool mirrors!" he said. And the two little Coons jumped off the log and rolled about laughing. They thought it was so funny that they ran off to tell their mother.

Smiling Pool was not a big pool. But it looked big to those two little Coons for they had never seen so much water at one time. At first, all that water scared them a little. But Mother left them to play on the bank while she went farther on to try to catch some frogs, and little by little the two Coons crept nearer to the water, until they were right at the edge. They both washed their hands in it. The water was no longer so scary.

Then the two Coons saw a big log lying at the water's edge. They both ran out on it. Spiketail stood at one end of the log and Little Bob stood at the other end. There wasn't a ripple on the water and it was as smooth as a looking-glass. It was like a mirror.

Spiketail leaned over and looked down. He was startled to see a little Coon whom he had never seen before, looking up at him. At the same

THEIR FIRST BATH
THE MIRROR IN THE POOL

SPIKETAIL COON was called Spiketail because the end of his tail was a little more pointed than tails of other young Coons. One day Spiketail and his brother Little Bob went with their mother to make their first visit to the Smiling Pool.

When they left their home in the hole of a big hollow tree, Mother went down first, and the two young Coons followed her. The Coons were still babies, but they felt very big and important on this first trip away from home.

It had been fun to wet their hands and feet in the water as they passed by Laughing Brook. But when they arrived at Smiling Pool, both youngsters ran out on a log lying close to the water's edge. The water in Smiling Pool did not ripple and run over pebbles and stones as Laughing Brook did. The water in Smiling Pool was quiet and still.

FAIR EXCHANGES

Notice how freely many members of Mother Nature's family help one another. You will see that without that help, many forms of life would die and disappear forever. The oxygen in the air which animals must have in order to live, is supplied by the plants and trees. But when the animals exhale the air from their lungs, it contains a kind of gas, called carbonic acid, which is necessary to the life of the plant. So, you see, neither the plants nor the animals could live their natural lives without the other.

Butterflies and bees live on the nectar of flowers, but in getting this nectar they also gather on their legs and bodies the fertilizing powder, called pollen. This they take to the next blossom, where it will cause the growth of the seed which will produce another plant. The insect pays well for its meals by keeping alive the plants from which it gets its food.

The Handy-Footed Owl

Of all the birds (and the animals, too, excepting the monkeys and the apes and parrots) the owls are the handiest with their feet, and if you don't see how any creature can be *handy* with its *feet,* that's just because you don't know about owls—and apes. For when an owl perches, he has two of the toes on each foot in *front* and two *behind,* which gives him the strongest possible grip. But when he pounces on his prey, his toes point to the four quarters of a circle, which position gives him the best hold. And again, when he alights on the ground, he puts three toes in front and one behind, the best position for walking. Can you make your fingers do so many different things?

AUTUMN

THE LANDSCAPE. PAINTED IN BRILLIANT COLORS! THE
FRAGRANCE OF RIPENED FRUITS! FEATHERED HOSTS WING
SOUTH. THE BLESSED SEASON OF HARVEST AND THANKSGIVING.

Who Paints the Leaves?

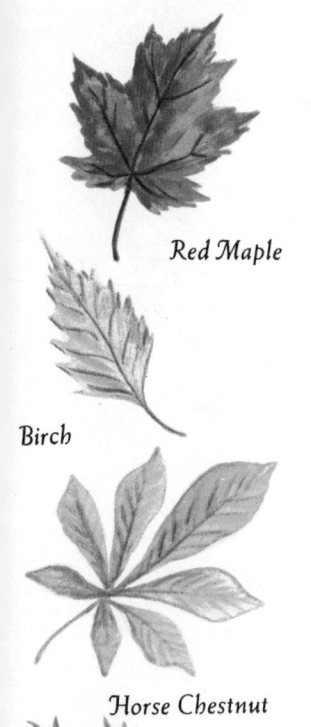

Red Maple

Birch

Horse Chestnut

Scarlet Oak

SOME folks tell us that it is Jack Frost who paints the leaves in the autumn. It is then that the green leaves turn into the beautiful reds and yellows and browns that you love to look at. But other people tell us that it isn't Jack Frost at all who paints the leaves. These wise men tell us a different reason why the leaves change color in the fall.

In the summer time when the trees are full of life and strength, their leaves are green. At this time they contain a great deal of a certain substance called chlorophyll (pronounced klo-ro-fill), which gives them their green color. The summer work of the trees is to give shade and to help purify the air.

In the autumn, when this work is done, the green substance begins to run out of the leaves through the stems. It runs into the wood of the twigs and branches. But it leaves behind a yellow substance which had been hidden in the green, and also other substances which turn red in the cooler air.

That is why the red and yellow colors are brightest and most beautiful when the cool Autumn nights follow warm days.

So, you see, everybody is right. If it is Jack Frost who makes the nights cool, then he helps turn the leaves yellow and red and brown.

White Oak

Beech

White Poplar

Sugar Maple

At first the cubs couldn't figure out what their mother was doing. She was part way up a dead tree. She had made an opening in the tree big enough to put her paw in. She would pull out a pawful of something and eat it. Then she would lick her paw, and they could hear her grunting with pleasure. And all the time there was a humming sound, an angry hum.

The sound came from the bees, who were angry because Mother Bear was eating their golden honey. Just then a big piece of honeycomb, dripping with honey, fell down right near the two little bears. They sniffed at it. Then they tasted. A Bee stung Teeny, but he didn't even know it. They forgot everything but this wonderful new food. They even forgot they had disobeyed Mother. And as Mother Bear dropped down more pieces of honeycomb, she forgot it, too. You see, Mother Bear was just as happy with all the honey as they were.

TWO HAPPY LITTLE BEARS

TEENY BEAR and Weeny Bear were the liveliest babies in the Green Forest. There was no guessing what they would do next, and Mother Bear was sure they were the most mischievous. They often disobeyed their mother although they didn't mean to disobey. They would just forget. There is nothing so easy to do as to forget.

One day Mother Bear sent the cubs up a tree and told them to stay in it until she came back. At first the cubs stayed up in the tree, climbing around on the branches and chasing each other up and down. Then they forgot they were supposed to stay up in the tree, and scrambled down.

"Let's go find Mother," said Weeny Bear, and off they started to look for Mother Bear. They followed her footprints for a little way, then lost them. But at last, by good luck, they found her.

of plants instead of eating a few plants all the way down to the ground. That's why you have no business in this garden."

"Have you?" asked Peter pertly.

"I certainly have," retorted Old Mr. Toad promptly. "You don't see me being chased out of this garden as you are. I help take care of it. If I weren't around a lot of plants wouldn't have a chance to grow. They would be cut down close to the ground by caterpillars called Cutworms. But I go after the Cutworms and eat them. They remind me of you."

"How can worms remind you of me?" asked Peter.

"Because they spoil more than they eat!" Old Mr. Toad answered, with a twinkle in his eyes. "You eat to ruin a garden and I eat to save it. That's why I belong in this garden and you don't."

"But I'm here just the same," said Peter. Just then Flip, the Terrier, came down the garden path. Peter slipped under the fence, and lipperty, lipperty, lip—he was off.

Peter Rabbit and Mr. Toad

OLD MR. TOAD was back in Farmer Brown's garden after a nice little visit with his relatives at the Smiling Pool. Looking happily around the garden, he saw Peter Rabbit sitting just inside the fence.

"Hello, Longears!" said Old Mr. Toad. "What are you doing over here?" Peter Rabbit replied, "Oh, I just came to look around."

"You mean just to taste around," said Old Mr. Toad, and chuckled at his little joke.

"Oh, I might take a bite here and a bite there, just to find out how things taste," admitted Peter Rabbit. "It's a change from grass and clover, and a change is good for everybody."

"That's the trouble with you," said Old Mr. Toad severely. "You think you are not doing any harm to the garden, but you are. You eat a little here. You eat a little there. You eat a little somewhere else. You spoil a lot

So the four little Foxes did the same thing, although they saw no reason why they should.

Mrs. Jimmy and her six little ones paid no attention to the Foxes as they passed by. One young Fox, bolder than the others, crept up toward the last Skunk, as if to jump on him. "Stop!" barked Reddy sharply. The little Fox stopped.

"I'm not afraid of such a little fellow as that," muttered the little Fox. "I don't see any reason why we should have got out of their way. They should have got out of our way."

Reddy grinned. "You may not see the reason, but there is one. Never judge others by size alone. Skunks are not very big but each of them, even the little babies, have a scent gun. They can shoot out a very unpleasant smell." And so the little Foxes learned that a wise Fox will always be polite to a Skunk, big or little.

BE POLITE TO THE SKUNKS

REDDY FOX and Mrs. Reddy were teaching their four little Foxes how to catch grasshoppers. When the little ones became tired with running and jumping, Mother and Father decided that it was time to go home.

Just before reaching the Old Pasture, they met another grasshopper party. It was Mrs. Jimmy Skunk and her six children. All were dressed alike in black and white. They were following their mother one behind the other.

When Mrs. Jimmy saw the Fox family in front of her, she lifted her big, broad, black tail with a white tip, spread it, and held it up straight. All the little Skunks did the same.

Then Reddy Fox did something that caused the Fox cubs to stare in surprise. He most politely stepped aside. Mrs. Reddy also stepped aside.

SUMMER

COMES NOW THE SEASON OF WARMTH, OF FLOWERS AND BIRDS; THE SMELL OF NEW MOWN HAY; SUNNY AND HAZY DAYS; VACATION DAYS; FIRST FRUITS OF EARLY HARVEST.

Mourning Cloak Butterfly

Virgin Tiger Moth

Dog's Head Butterfly

Luna Moth

A Butterfly's Clothing

HAVE you ever touched a butterfly or moth? If you have, you found something on your fingers that looked like dust. But this is not really dust—it is the butterfly's clothing.

If you looked at some butterflies and moths through a microscope you would see that this dust on their wings is really tiny scales, arranged something like those on a fish, or the shingles on a roof. These scales are forms of hairs that grow wide instead of long.

They make the wings stronger and also give them their beautiful colors. If you rub off the butterfly's scales, these colors disappear.

Cottonwood Dagger Moth

Monarch Butterfly (small)

Sulphur Butterfly

Tiger Swallowtail Butterfly

Eastern Tailed Blue Butterfly

Polyphemus Moth

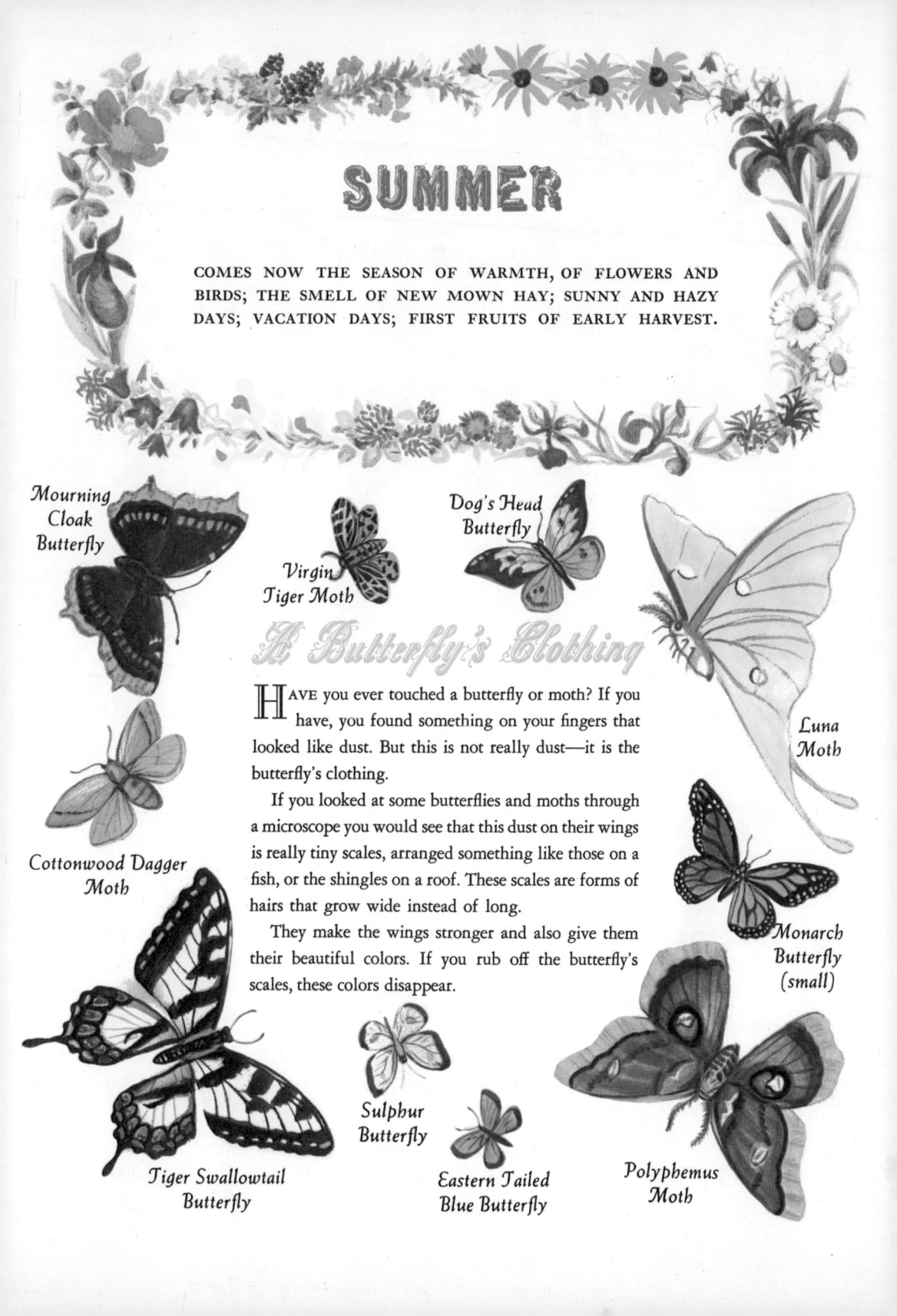

That settled the matter. There was no doubt now about it being time to get up. He crawled up his long hall and when he reached his doorway, he sat for a few minutes blinking at the light. When his eyes got used to the light so that he could see, he discovered Peter Rabbit sitting there with his back to him. His eyes twinkled with mischief. Taking the greatest care not to make the teeniest, weeniest sound he crept up behind him.

Peter was thinking about a story he had just heard when the sound of growls right at his very back made him jump. With a little scream he started for the old stone wall. There he turned to look. What he saw was someone rolling over and over with laughter. Peter's heart gave a great leap of gladness.

"Johnny Chuck!" he shouted, and started back as fast as he had come. "I'll get even with you some day, see if I don't, Johnny Chuck!" he cried as Johnny scrambled to his feet grinning broadly.

Then Peter began to ask questions. He wanted to know all about how it feels to sleep all winter and how Johnny ever learned to do it and a lot more foolish things. And Johnny Chuck couldn't answer one of them. Why? Because he didn't know. All he knew was that he had fallen asleep in the fall and now it was spring and he was awake again. What Johnny wanted to know was where he could find a breakfast.

Johnny Chuck's Spring Awakening

PETER RABBIT was sitting down in the far corner of the Old Orchard very near the doorstep of an old friend. Now the owner of that doorstep had been asleep ever since the first cold day of last fall. Curled up in bed in his snug, warm little bedroom, deep down in the ground, he had known nothing of snow and ice. He had slept through it all. But that morning sweet Mistress Spring had stopped at his doorway to waken him. When she heard him stretching and yawning and grumbling she went to waken others.

"I don't believe it is time to get up yet," he grumbled; "I don't believe I've been asleep any time at all." How Peter Rabbit would have shouted if he could have heard that.

But no one heard it because, you know, that little grumbler was way down in his snug bedroom under ground. Suddenly there broke a sound which caused him to sit very still and listen with all his might. It was the voice of Welcome Robin singing:

"Cheer up! Cheer up! Cheer up! Cheer!
Mistress Spring is surely here."

But Little Pete was just a very small Rabbit and his legs soon became tired. He sat down to rest. It was very still and quiet out there on the Green Meadows. For the first time in his short life he felt lonesome and wished he hadn't come.

Just then there was a frightful sound. It was a loud BOOM close behind him. His little heart seemed to jump right up in his throat. He was too frightened to think.

But he didn't need to think. His funny little long heels began working without his thinking. They took him over the grass, lipperty, lipperty, lip, twice as fast as he ever had run before. Because he had been looking back he was headed in the right direction.

Boom! That dreadful sound was right behind him again. With a few long leaps he reached the dear safe Old Briar-patch and crept under a bramble bush. "I'll never leave it again, I never, never will," he sobbed as he lay there panting for breath.

It was a long, long time before Little Pete learned that there really had been nothing to fear. It was one of his mother's feathered friends who had spied him out where he had no business to be, and so had frightened him home. It was Boomer the Nighthawk, who flies in the dusk and makes those loud booms by plunging from high in the air and suddenly stopping himself with his wings just in time not to strike the ground.

Little Pete never again thought he knew all there was to know.

One night Little Pete overheard his father telling his mother about a wonderful bed of sweet clover in the Green Meadows, some distance away. "It's the sweetest clover I've ever tasted," declared Father Peter.

The next day, Little Pete ran out to a small patch of clover near Old Briar-patch. He didn't intend to go beyond that. But as he sat there in the dusk, he remembered what he had overheard about that big bed of the sweetest clover his father had ever tasted. Right away he wanted to taste it too.

"Mother is just trying to keep us at home with all this talk about danger," thought little Pete. "It's all foolishness. I'm not afraid. I'm going out to find that big bed of clover. That's just what I'm going to do!"

He kicked up his funny little long heels and away he went, lipperty, lipperty, lip, just the way his father runs.

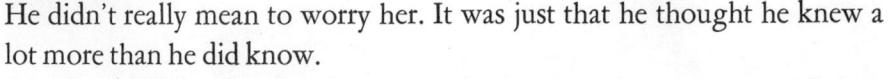

LITTLE PETE HAS A SCARE

HE was a wee little bunny, and he looked so much like his father, Peter Rabbit, that he was called Little Pete. Not only did he look like Peter but he was like him in other ways. He was full of curiosity. He was willful, wanting to have his own way. Mother had to watch him to keep him out of trouble. He didn't really mean to worry her. It was just that he thought he knew a lot more than he did know.

Little Pete had two sisters and a brother just his own age. All four bunnies had been warned over and over again never to go outside the dear, safe Old Briar-patch unless their mother or father was with them. But when Mother's back was turned, Little Pete would poke his wobbly little nose outside. He would run out a little way, snatch a leaf of sweet clover and scamper back as fast as his little legs would take him. At such times, he would feel very brave and very bold. This made the clover taste sweeter.

SPRING

THIS IS THE SEASON OF MAPLE-SUGAR, OF THE COMING OF WINSOME BLUEBIRD AND WELCOME ROBIN, AND OF THE BLOOMING OF THE FIRST BLOSSOMS OF THE YEAR.

SPRING GOSSIP

LISTEN! From the top of the tallest tree Welcome Robin is singing "Cheer up! Cheer up! Cheer up, cheer!" His heart is filled almost to bursting with the joy of spring.

Striped Chipmunk is whisking about as pert and saucy as ever. He still has some supplies in his storehouse and is a living proof of the value of thrift.

Glory the Cardinal is there too, whistling "Good cheer! Good cheer! Good cheer!"

Jerry Muskrat has moved from his house on the edge of the Smiling Pool to his castle in the bank because the water is rising so fast that he fears his house may be swept away. Jerry is taking no chances.

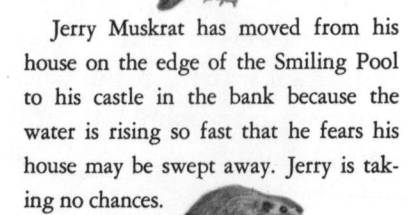

And over there in the Old Orchard is Tommy Tit. There is no mistaking his "Chickadee-dee! See me! See me!"

Roughleg the Hawk has left the Green Meadows for the North, and Danny Meadow Mouse says it is too good to be true.

Johnny Chuck hasn't appeared yet but he is expected almost any day now. Johnny doesn't know a thing about the hard winter we have had. Peter Rabbit says he's lucky.

Redwing the Blackbird says he has found no better place than the Smiling Pool and the Green Meadows, and will build among the bulrushes there as usual.

BURGESSVILLE, U.S.A.

Old Briar Patch

Green Meadow

Old Orchard

Johnny Woodchuck's
Home

Old Man Coyote's
Home

Reddy, the Fox's Home

Digger, the Badger's
Home

Old Unc' Possum's
Tree

Prickly Porcupine's
Log

Little Joe Otter's
Home

Henhouse

Farmer Brown's House

Corn Field

Danny Meadow
Mouse's Home

The Old   Pasture

Jimmy Skunk's
Home

Lightfoot, the Deer's Home

Beaver Dam

Sammy Jay's Home

Green Forest

Bobby Coon's
Tree

Jerry Muskrat's
Home

Shadow, the Weasel's
Home

Old Hickory Tree

Blacky Crow's Home

Hooty Owl's Tree

Happy Jack Squirrel's Home

Smiling Pool

Grandfather Frog's
Lily Pad

Big
Rock

Little Joe Otter's
Slide

Buster Bear's
Windfall

STORIES AROUND THE YEAR

Illustrated By Phoebe Erickson

GROSSET & DUNLAP • Publishers • NEW YORK